THE CHEF'S CUTIE

THE RIVER HILL SERIES

REBECCA NORINNE

JAMAILA BRINKLEY

For Jamaila, my partner in crime. WE WROTE FIVE BOOKS TOGETHER!

For Becky, who once said, "Hey, what if we wrote a book together?"

*Take a final trip to River Hill, where the kitchen isn't the
only place where things are heating up.*

Chef Max Vergaras's culinary star is rising, but when
his orphaned niece comes to live with him, expanding
his restaurant empire is put on the back burner. He's ill
equipped to handle raising a nine year old, especially
under the watchful eye of Elizabeth Teague, the social

services caseworker assigned to them. His life has never been more complicated, which includes his feelings for the blonde beauty: she's everything he wants—and everything he can't have. And since Lizzie holds his family's future in the palm of her hand, all of his thoughts about how she fits seamlessly into his life need to go on the back burner, too. Just as soon as he figures out how to get her out of his dreams.

Lizzie Teague has an important job to do, and she can't get distracted by one case—even if Mia's uncle Max has a way with food that has her thinking about things that definitely aren't on the menu. But with her career and reputation on the line, she has to remember why she took this job in the first place ... and it certainly wasn't to fall in love with her clients. No matter how loveable the sexy, charismatic chef and his sweet, young niece might be. So she'll keep her mind on the job and out of the gutter—just as soon as she can get her heart on board with that plan.

Max and Lizzie could lose everything if they give in to temptation. But what if it's possible for them to gain even more? What would they risk when love—and family—is on the line?

1
———

"Legal guardian?" The words came out much higher pitched than he intended. Max Vergaras was not normally a man who yelped.

The lawyer sitting across from him nodded. "Yes, Mr. Vergaras. Your sister's will is very clear."

Max gulped, sparing a glance to the other occupant of his living room. Nine-year-old Mia was outwardly absorbed in whatever she was carefully drawing in the notebook that seemingly never left her side, but Max suspected she was listening to their conversation very carefully.

In some ways, she was so much like his sister Isabel that every time he looked at her face he felt as though he was gasping for breath, his heart squeezing tight under the weight of memories and grief.

In other ways, Mia was a complete mystery to him —and had been just as much a mystery to her mother, he suspected. Mia was quiet and observant, where Isabel had been boisterous and spontaneous; shy where her mother had been outgoing. And of course, Mia had somehow inherited the true artistic talent that Isabel had craved, spent her whole life chasing, but never quite captured.

Which reminded him.

"What about—" he canted the upper half of his body forward, lowering his voice so that the lawyer had to lean in to hear him. "Her father?"

The other man shook his head. "There's no mention of it in any of her estate documents, sir. And they're very thorough."

Max frowned, distracted. "Isabel? Thorough?" He'd been surprised enough to discover that his sister had a will at all, let alone to discover it was finely-tuned and incredibly detailed.

The lawyer coughed. "Um, I'm probably not supposed to mention it, but Ms. Vergaras was, ahem, *acquainted* with one of our other clients. I believe it was on his recommendation that she set up the documents."

Max closed his eyes briefly, translating the lawyer's

coded statement easily enough. His sister had been dating somebody rich, and had actually taken someone else's advice for once. It must have been love.

"Is your, uh, client mentioned in the will?" Had the mystery man still been involved with Isabel? Was some boyfriend of hers going to show up when Max least expected? Timing-wise, the boyfriend couldn't be Mia's father, whoever *that* was. In his most private thoughts, Max suspected Isabel didn't know, either.

His sister had toted her baby around Southern California for years, following her whims from gig to gig. But when Mia had reached school age, Isabel had taken a position as the on-site manager of an artists' commune in Arizona, putting Mia in a private school run by a group who believed children should be educated exclusively in the outdoors. It had been the longest Isabel had stayed in one place since their parents had died. Silently, Max wondered if his sister had been getting restless again. If that was why she'd decided to go out on that motorcycle the day she died.

He shook his head slightly. He'd had plenty of time to think about that on the flight down to Arizona, plenty of time to let his thoughts circle helplessly. Now he and Mia were home in River Hill, and from the sound of things, it was going to be permanent. Which was something he'd have to think about later, he realized, as the lawyer continued speaking. He tried to pay attention again.

"You're the only one mentioned at all in the will,

Mr. Vergaras. Your sister was quite specific that you be her daughter's sole legal guardian. Her remaining assets were left to Miss Mia under your discretion."

"Assets?" Isabel hadn't had any assets that he'd been aware of. She'd spent the last of her trust fund from their parents getting herself and Mia to Arizona. For his part, Max had spent his on culinary school, and the last of it, carefully hoarded, had helped him buy out the previous owner of Frankie's, his beloved restaurant. But Isabel had used hers to live the life of a perpetual student, taking any art class that struck her fancy, and supplementing the trust with gigs as a roadie, or a personal assistant, or once even as a makeup artist. How she'd bluffed her way into that one, Max had no idea, but he'd enjoyed the pictures she'd sent periodically.

"There isn't much, I'm afraid—" The lawyer sounded apologetic, as though Max deserved more from his dead sister. Maybe the man regularly encountered relatives who got angry about this sort of thing. Max, however, mostly felt numb. He glanced at Mia, who had barely said two words to him in the last forty-eight hours. "There is the retirement account, of course," the lawyer continued.

"The what?"

The man looked down at his papers. "Er... the 401K?"

"Isabel had a 401K?" That had to be a mistake.

"Yes, sir. Small, but robustly invested, if I may say so."

Max scrubbed his hands against his face, feeling stubble rasp along his palms. "Okay. I don't—" He paused, and took a deep breath. "Honestly, I don't really care about the assets. Can you just send whatever you need to send over to my lawyer?" He reached for the documents and pen the older man was holding out, and scribbled Ben Worthington's name and phone number at the top. Thank god for childhood friends.

"Very good, sir, I'll do that. There's just the matter of the guardianship, then."

"What about my grandparents?" Max blurted, hating how desperate he sounded. He loved his niece. Adored her. But how could *he* raise a kid? "Wouldn't a, uh, stable couple be better for her?"

The lawyer's voice was dry when he answered. "Even if your sister's will didn't specifically lay out her intentions, Mr. Vergaras, I'm afraid that even a bachelor uncle is a better proposition than a pair of ninety-year-olds who live in another country."

He winced. "Ah. Right." Abi and Belo wouldn't thank him for disrupting their quiet life by foisting their great-granddaughter off on them. They no longer travelled, of course, so the frequent visits he remembered from his childhood were a thing of the past. He flew to see them occasionally, but he didn't think Isabel had seen them in years. Which probably meant Mia didn't know them at all. He'd have to get her down to

Argentina to see them before too much more time went by. Abi and Belo were all either of them had left.

"Of course, CPS will assign you a caseworker," the lawyer added almost as an afterthought.

"A what?"

"The department of child welfare?" The other man raised his eyebrows. "In cases like this, CPS will assign a social worker to the child to ensure that she is being properly cared for. You know, since there wasn't a previously established residential relationship."

"A previous—Oh, you mean she's never lived with me?"

The lawyer nodded, and then his face softened as he glanced at Mia. "If I may be blunt, Mr. Vergaras. I understand that you own a restaurant?"

"Yes, Frankie's."

"Mmm-hmm, yes. Well, this transition may be difficult for you, sir, but I strongly advise you to put the child's well-being first."

Max straightened. "Are you implying I wouldn't?"

The other man sighed. "From what I understand, she's had a somewhat untraditional upbringing. Flinging her into the public school system, even in a welcoming town like River Hill, is going to be a challenge for her. And she'll need you to be around." He leaned forward. "Look, sir, my brother-in-law owns a Denny's. He's busy all the time. I know the comparison might not be quite on par—"

"I should think not," Max said stiffly. A *Denny's*!

The lawyer plowed on. "All I mean to say is your schedule, and her schedule, may not line up well. You're going to have to think about things like child care, and homework assistance, and social events—"

Social events? "She's nine!" Max protested.

"My nine year old has a cell phone," the lawyer told him without missing a beat.

Max slid back into the cool leather embrace of the couch and held in a moan. "Oh, god."

"All I'm saying, sir, is that CPS isn't your enemy. You can ask the caseworker for help and resources."

"If I do that, they'll think I can't handle her." He sat up straight again as a terrible thought came to him. "If they take her away from me, where would she go?"

"Foster care." The answer was delivered in Mia's soft voice. She hadn't looked up from her notebook, and her pencil was still moving carefully across the page.

There was a moment of silence as Max and the lawyer exchanged guarded glances.

"How do you know?" Max finally asked.

Mia shrugged, still not meeting his eyes. "Mom had CPS out a few times. Sometimes the artists didn't approve of a kid on the grounds. Or they thought they knew better than she did about how I should be raised."

The lawyer winced visibly. Apparently this particular nine-year-old knew exactly what 'untraditional upbringing' meant.

"You're not going to foster care," Max said firmly. "We'll figure this out. I can do this." He successfully ran a restaurant staffed mostly by miscreants and ne'er-do-wells who he'd somehow managed to turn into a well-oiled, award-winning machine. He had the James Beard certificate hanging on his wall to prove it, for heaven's sake! How hard could one young girl be?

The lawyer began to sort through his paperwork. "I'll just need your signature in a few places, Mr. Vergaras, to confirm you understand everything we've discussed, and to set the guardianship process in motion."

"There's a process?"

"It's not hard," the man assured him. "Particularly since it was set out in your sister's will, and you're consenting to it." He paused. "You are consenting, right?"

Max scowled at him. "Of course I'm consenting."

The man cracked a small smile for the first time his entire visit. "Welcome to fatherhood, sir. I'm sure you'll enjoy it. It's the most rewarding—"

"All right. Just show me where to sign." Max scribbled his name on the papers without reading much of anything, something Ben would have his head for later.

"Thank you, sir. I'll be sending these through CPS so that they can pass them up to the judge to sign off on."

"Wait. CPS has something to do with it? I thought they were just going to check up on me periodically."

"Well, they have to approve your living situation, Mr. Vergaras. And make sure that everything's safe for the child…" The lawyer trailed off, his eyes flicking toward the giant TV that took up most of the living room wall.

"What, nine year olds can't watch football?"

"Um… I'm not the expert, sir. You'll want to consult your caseworker on what's appropriate—and what's not."

Max did a quick mental inventory of his home and frowned. It wasn't like Mia was a toddler. Was he going to have to store his beloved chef's knives in a drawer or something?

Meanwhile, the lawyer was looking wide-eyed at the glass-doored mini-fridges tucked on either side of the entertainment center. One held unlabeled bottles of craft beer that Max was testing for a friend who was hoping to launch his own brewery at some point in the future. The other contained bottles of his friend Noah Bradstone's latest bottling of chardonnay. Not to mention the bottles of Ben's girlfriend Maeve Brennan's whiskey lined up neatly on the bar he'd built along the wall next to the door to the kitchen. Come to think of it, everything in here was supplied by one friend or another. With a kid in the house, he was probably going to have to find a friend who owned a dairy. Kids drank a lot of milk, right?

"I'll see what I can do," he told the lawyer.

Finally, the man gathered up all of the papers Max had signed and tucked them into a folder inside his briefcase. "Thank you for your time, Mr. Vergaras. And I'm very sorry for your loss." He slid a glance toward Mia. "For yours as well, Miss Mia." The gesture set him several bars higher on Max's personal ladder. Nearly everyone he'd spoken with over the last two days had ignored Mia, speaking only to him, as if it weren't her life being affected the most. Sure, he'd lost the sister he loved, but Mia had lost her *mother*.

His mind strayed back to when his own parents had died before he quickly shut those memories down and locked them away in the deepest recesses of his mind. He didn't have time for the kind of all-consuming grief that had shattered his world. He'd failed his sister back then, and so many times since, but he wasn't about to fail her daughter now.

He could do this dad thing. In fact, he was going to *fucking crush it*.

After walking the lawyer to the door, he returned to the living room to stare at the new center of his world. Mia, for her part, continued to ignore him. He blew out a breath before silently turning away and heading toward his office down the hall to make some important calls. Frankie's had been without him for two days now; he was going to have to get back to work soon. In the meantime, he needed some help. He picked up the phone and dialed his best friend's number.

"Ben? Yeah, I'm back. You're going to be getting some papers from a lawyer to look over. And, uh, I guess I need some help re-doing the guest room." He sat down heavily in his chair and heroically resisted the urge to put his head in his hands. "Also, what can you tell me about CPS requirements?"

2

*L*izzie Teague closed the manila folder containing all the pertinent information for today's home visit and shoved it back inside her leather satchel. She checked her reflection in the rearview mirror one final time, pushing some wayward wisps of blonde hair back into the tight bun at the nape of her neck, and made her way up the long gravel walkway toward her client's front door.

Normally, she would have met Mr. Vergaras and his niece Mia for the first time in her office, but with this case being an interstate transfer that had only landed on her desk that morning, she was playing

catch-up straight out of the gate. So a home visit
it was.

Still, she had a good feeling about this case. Well,
as good a feeling as you could have when a young girl
had just lost her only parent and had been sent to live
with a bachelor uncle she barely knew. But a quick bit
of Googling had showed Mr. Vergaras to be a man with
deep ties to his community, something Mia had been
lacking while living with her mother. He owned a
popular local restaurant, and was frequently
mentioned in various news articles for charitable
giving and community event participation. On paper,
he seemed like a good guy. For the girl's sake, she
hoped he was just as good in real life. It was her job to
find out.

She raised her hand to knock on the door, but
before her knuckles could hit the wood, it swung open,
revealing a wall of tall, dark masculinity. She'd seen a
picture of Max Vergaras in her files, of course, but it
had done nothing to highlight just how truly gorgeous
the man actually was. With his tanned skin, lean
muscles, and black hair that had a subtle wave—in
other words, *exactly her type*—there was no denying he
was one of the most handsome men she'd ever laid
eyes on.

*Which is a completely inappropriate thought to be
having about one of my clients*, she inwardly chided
herself—even as she fought to pull her gaze away from
his full lower lip. *Do your job, girl.*

"Oh, you're here." He glanced down at his watch and then raised his eyes back up, his brows pinched with annoyance. "Your office said you wouldn't be by until later this afternoon. I wasn't expecting you yet."

Lizzie stifled a frustrated sigh. She loved her job—really, she did. The office she worked out of was a different story, though. Her boss had severe control issues, which would have been fine if she wasn't also a scatterbrain who often forgot to pass along important information to her caseworkers (or, as Lizzie sometimes speculated, kept it from them purposely). It seemed to her that more often than not—by design or accident, she couldn't say—the right hand didn't know what the left was doing. The families she worked with were already stressed out and fearful, and having their chains yanked by the people who were supposedly there to help them did nothing to inspire confidence.

"I'm sorry, no." She stood up straighter, hoping to project an air of authority. At just a smidge over five feet tall, it was an action she employed when interacting with big men who might attempt to intimidate her. Sometimes it helped, and sometimes it didn't, but she wasn't taking any chances. Especially not with Mr. Vergaras's obvious irritation practically radiating off him in waves, a scowl pulling his handsome face into a stern frown.

He blew out a long, slow breath and shook his head before stepping aside to let her enter. "Come on in, then. I have to warn you, though, the place is a mess. We were hoping to clean up a bit before you got here."

"We?" Lizzie asked as he led her through the slate-tiled foyer and into a wide open great room that was a combined living, dining, and kitchen space. "Is there a Mrs. Vergaras I wasn't made aware of?" As her eyes continued to scan the room, she reached into the bag at her hip, worried that she'd accidentally overlooked that important detail. She didn't often make that sort of mistake, but she also didn't often get a new case with shoddy paperwork dumped in her lap with only a few hours notice the way this one had been.

Mr. Vergaras leaned his hip against the leather sectional, gesturing with his thumb over his shoulder toward a long hallway that led in the opposite direction. "No, no wife. I was talking about Mia, but we seem to have very different ideas about what constitutes tidying up. According to her, this *is* clean." He scanned the room briefly with flattened lips before his eyes found hers again.

Lizzie held back a chuckle. It was wrong to laugh at the man, but if he honestly thought this was messy, he was in for a rude awakening. There was a throw blanket on the sofa that wasn't folded, and a stack of young adult novels on the coffee table, but otherwise, the room was fairly tidy and well put together. For a bachelor pad. Something they'd have to discuss before she left. "Sir—"

"Please, call me Max," he interrupted. "I hate being

called sir. It makes me feel so old." For the first time since he'd opened his front door, he smiled.

And Lizzie's knees nearly buckled. Good lord. This man wasn't just handsome. He was—

NO.

Inwardly, she shook her head to dislodge those thoughts. Max Vergaras was Mia's guardian, not some guy she'd met ... well, nowhere. Because she never went out. But that was neither here nor there. Regardless of how hot he was, she needed to keep things professional.

But damn, his smile—when it happened—was like the clouds had parted, leaving the sun to beam down on her from the heavens. The traces of gray in his lush black hair only added to his attractiveness, and that dimple that popped in his right cheek? Whew! Max Vergaras was a staggeringly attractive specimen of manhood.

And he is completely off limits, she reminded herself sternly. She needed to get her act together. Her job was far more important than her neglected lady parts, no matter what her libido was howling at her.

She cleared her throat. "Do you mind if we sit, Max? I'd like to go over what you can expect from social services in the coming weeks, and the role I'll be playing in finalizing your custody arrangement. And before I leave, I'd also like to speak with Mia in private, if you don't mind."

"Of course not." He gestured to the oversized

leather sofa that took up a large portion of the living room area. "Is here good?"

"Thank you," Lizzie said, settling down into one of the couch's surprisingly comfortable cushions before pulling a pad of paper and pen from her bag.

"First, how close were you and Isabel?"

Pain flashed in Max's eyes as he rubbed his palm across his forehead. "Not as close as I would have wanted these past few years. Isabel was a rolling stone, while I like my roots to run a bit deeper, if you get my meaning."

Lizzie nodded. "You've lived in River Hill for nearly ten years, right? And from the look of things, you don't have plans of going anywhere else anytime soon."

"That's right," he answered. "I rented an apartment near Frankie's for the first couple of years I was here, but I bought this place five years ago. I figured … well, never mind what I figured." He shrugged. "Anyhow, River Hill is my home now." His tone was both wistful and proud. Almost like he'd hoped to have someone to share the house with, but his bachelorhood didn't lessen the accomplishment of buying it any.

In a way, Lizzie could commiserate. While she didn't own a big, beautiful mid-century modern house like Max did, she remembered with pride the day her realtor had passed her the keys for her small town-home thirty minutes south of here. At the time, she'd thought of it as a starter home, something she'd build equity in until she got married and moved into *their* starter home. Seven years later, she was no closer to finding someone to marry, much less buy a house with.

"Speaking of River Hill," Lizzie said, shuffling the papers in her lap. "Have you decided which school Mia will attend? There's the local public elementary school, of course, but the Catholic school down the road has an excellent reputation."

Max shoved his hands through his hair with a small groan and leaned back against the sofa back. "Mia wants to go to the Catholic school," he said, dropping his palms onto his thick, muscled thighs.

After a quick moment spent appreciating the way he filled out his jeans, Lizzie dragged her eyes back up to his face. "You seem ... perturbed by that?"

He shot her a look that she had trouble interpreting. A big part of what made her so good at her job was being able to read people. Understand what they *weren't* saying. It was unusual for her not to be able to immediately place what he was thinking.

"I'm an atheist."

"Ah," she hummed.

"Yeah. Ah."

In her line of work, she didn't often come across adoptive guardians who so readily admitted their aversion to religion. If anything, they often *exaggerated* their devotion in an effort to impress her—as if going to church was the only requirement to being a good, stable guardian or parent. Two years ago she'd been forced to remove two young kids from a home where their foster parent quoted from the bible while hitting them with a switch fashioned from a branch from the tree in their backyard.

"Was your sister religious, then?" she asked, pushing that horrible memory to the side.

Max laughed and shook his head. "Religious? Not in the least. Spiritual? Very much so. In fact, the last time I spoke with her—" he tripped over the word, his eyes falling closed as he swallowed deeply, his adam's apple bobbing in his throat. After a few seconds, he opened his eyes back up, and the pure grief Lizzie saw in them reached straight into her chest and tugged at her heartstrings. "Last month, she told me about a chakra cleansing ritual she'd planned to undertake with a shaman who was visiting the commune where she lived."

And Mia wanted to go to Catholic school? That seemed ... odd, Lizzie thought. But then she had another thought. "Would you call your niece's upbringing unconventional?"

Max raised an eyebrow. "You heard the part about the shaman, right?"

Lizzie fought a smile. And failed. "Yes, I did." She forced her lips back into a flat, uninterested line. "And based on your knowledge of your sister and her lifestyle, would you say that extended to Mia's schooling as well?"

Max gripped the back of his neck. "I ..." He blew out a breath. "I don't know much about that, if I'm being honest. Isabel was always vague when I asked, and when I tried to talk to Mia about it the other day, she just stared at me. It was kind of unnerving, actually."

"Unnerving how?" Lizzie asked, making a note in her files.

Max pitched forward, resting his elbows on his thighs, his fingers linked between his knees. He twisted his face around to stare at Lizzie, and she had to remind herself not to drool. "I don't think it's any surprise to anyone at your agency that I don't have much experience with kids. I'm a thirty-five-year old single man, and none of my friends have kids. Isabel is my only sister, and she lived a plane ride away. All that said, I've always found kids ... excitable. Hyperactive. At least, that's how I was at her age. And Isabel was infinitely worse. But every time I try to talk with Mia, she just sits there staring at me. When I finish saying whatever it is I was saying, she answers politely, using as few words as possible. Honestly, she's the chillest fucking person I've ever met—pardon my French." He winced at his use of the expletive, and his eyes darted down to where Lizzie held her pen.

She smiled at him placatingly. "Don't worry, Mr. Ver—"

"Max, please."

She set her pen and paper to the side. "I'm not going to report you for swearing, but it's probably best if you don't make a habit of it, especially around Mia. Children her age are highly impressionable."

He blew out a breath. "I'm not so sure about that one."

Lizzie tilted her head to the side. "What do you mean?"

"I mean my sister was a handful. I loved her —*adored her*—but she was a force to be reckoned with. Our parents used to call her Hurricane Isabel. Mia looks like a miniature version of my sister, but in every other way, she's the complete opposite. I highly doubt she's going to take up cursing anytime soon. At this point, I might even welcome a well-timed fuck or two —at least then I'd know she was processing her grief."

Lizzie weighed her next words. Not all of the families she encountered were open to hearing about her personal experiences. "Can I be frank with you, Max?"

"Please do," he said, sounding almost relieved.

"My parents died in a car accident when I was ten, and I went to live with my Uncle Jonathan and his partner Horatio. So I have some experience with being a young girl dealing with the traumatic loss of her parents. What's more, I also know what it's like to be thrust upon relatives who were not prepared to deal with my grief, let alone raising me. What Mia's going through isn't unusual, but she'll need extra care."

Max let out a long gust of air. "I'm sorry, I didn't know."

"We met an hour ago. There's no way you would have."

He was rubbing his palms up and down his jean-clad thighs. "I'm going to screw this up, aren't I?"

Lizzie felt the right side of her lips lifting in a small smile. "Probably. All parents do, in one way or another."

"Fuck," he breathed out, then winced again. "Sorry."

"It's going to be okay, Max." Without conscious thought, she leaned forward and set her hand on his forearm. When her palm connected with his skin, it tingled with a sort of buzzing, electric warmth. She sucked in a surprised gasp and pulled it quickly away.

Max's tongue darted out and he licked his bottom lip. "Ms. Teague ..."

"Please, call me Lizzie," she said, gratified to hear her voice sounding much more steady than her rapidly beating heart.

He swallowed. "I ..." His gaze dropped down to where she'd touched him and then slowly back up. When he met her eyes, she couldn't miss the unmistakable heat in his stare, but she could see him trying hard to restrain it, too. Which was what she should be doing, as well. A few beats passed in silence before Max suddenly pushed to his feet. "Come on. Let me introduce you to Mia."

Lizzie stood and hefted her bag over her shoulder and across her body. "Yeah, that'd be great." And not just because she needed to put as much space between them as she could before she threw herself at him. Besides, she had some theories about Mia's reaction to her uncle, and her request about school that she wanted to discuss with the girl.

"Follow me."

Lizzie did as requested, telling herself the entire walk down the long hallway not to stare at his hard, firm ass. She managed to only look twice.

3

The first disaster came far more quickly than Max had expected. He sat frowning over the registration forms for St. Aloysius, wondering just how he'd been talked into sending his free-spirited sister's child to Catholic school. He blamed the caseworker from CPS.

She'd been nothing like what he'd expected. For one thing, she'd been fucking gorgeous. And there had been an unmistakable flare of heat in her eyes when she'd looked him up and down. He'd found himself wanting to drag her inside the house and push her up against the wall and discover just how those lush lips of hers tasted.

Surprising, since he hadn't felt that way about a woman since Vanessa.

Possibly not even about Vanessa, if he thought about it. She'd been great in bed and he'd genuinely adored her—the ring buried in his safe deposit box for the last five years showed just how much he'd been ready to be with her forever—but when she'd left him for her ex-husband's former best friend, he hadn't tried to get her back. Later, Noah had told him he wasn't surprised when she'd left. Max had tried to make a real effort to act offended, because the truth was that deep down, he wasn't all that surprised, either. Honestly, he suspected he wasn't really cut out for relationships.

Sex, though, *that* he was cut out for. And Lizzie Teague's lithe body on his front step had reminded him just how little of it he'd been having lately. Pretty much since business at Frankie's had picked up and the franchise offers had started coming in.

Of all the people for his sleeping libido to wake up for, the caseworker who could take Mia away from him with a snap of her manicured fingers was the worst possible choice.

He shook his head and stared down at the forms. He had to stop thinking about her. Or rather, he had to stop thinking about her naked. Keeping her fully-clothed form in mind as he tried to balance all of this new stuff was probably a good idea. His legal status as Mia's sole guardian wasn't final yet, and Lizzie Teague had a lot to do with whether it would be. He had to do this right.

Except he had no idea what the answers to most of these school registration questions were. He didn't know Mia's social security number. Had she ever been hospitalized or had surgery? What were her medication allergies? Dental history? Why did they need to know that? Did *he* need to know that? He made his way down the form, filling in what he could as panic slowly churned in his belly.

His pen hovered over the lines earmarked for Mia's emergency contacts. They probably meant people other than him, right? His information was all over the top of the form. And underneath 'Emergency Contacts' was another line for 'Authorized to Pick Up.' What did that mean? Were they different? Not having the faintest clue if he was doing this right, he scribbled the names of several friends in each section, and, as an afterthought, added Ms. Teague as well. That was probably a responsible thing to do, right? Then he set to hunting through the paperwork the lawyer had given him to find Mia's social security number, at the very least.

"I'VE GOT THIS, UNCLE MAX." Mia tugged the backpack

out of his hands, the new material crinkling as she swung it over her shoulder.

He'd taken her to Target at his friend Angelica's suggestion—the former actress had a serious love affair with the store—and bought everything on the list of supplies the school had sent over, plus everything Mia even hinted at liking. When they'd come home and he'd texted Angelica a picture of the pile of bags on the living room floor, she'd sent back an eyeroll emoji and a comment about how throwing money at things wasn't always the right answer. But Mia had given him a shy smile as she'd hung up the cardigan with a sequined owl on it in her closet, and he'd become overwhelmed with confidence again.

Now, though, he watched the bus roll to a stop in front of the house and bit the inside of his lip to keep from babbling reassurances at Mia. She gave him a one-armed hug, then took a deep breath and went utterly still for a few moments as the bus doors opened. Before he could say anything, though, she was moving, walking up the steps quietly, nodding hello to the driver's cheerful greeting and disappearing behind the tinted windows as she took a seat. The doors closed, the bus moved, and she was gone, away from him for the first time since she'd arrived.

He blew out a long breath and went back inside to gather his own things.

The rest of his day felt almost normal—answering emails, placing orders, interviewing a new server—

until halfway through afternoon prep, when his phone rang.

"Mr. Vergaras? This is Sheryl from the office at St. Aloysius."

He'd never really believed you could feel your heart dropping out of your chest, but his had clearly just fallen onto the restaurant floor. He glanced down involuntarily, sure there would be a bloody organ at his feet. "Yes?"

"I have Mia in the office with me, Mr. Vergaras. She's missed her bus and needs a pickup."

His brain went utterly blank for a moment. "Ah … I—"

"When can we expect you, sir?"

He swallowed and glanced around at his busy kitchen, the checklist at his own station half-completed. "Thirty minutes." He was already untying his apron as he hung up the phone and yelled for his sous chef.

Thirty-two minutes later he pulled into the parking lot at St. Aloysius and collected Mia from Sheryl, who looked down her nose at him.

"What happened?" he asked when they got to the car.

"I didn't know what bus number to go to," Mia said as she buckled herself in. "I'm sorry."

"It's okay," he answered. "I guess I should have written it down somewhere, because I don't know, either."

"Mrs. Hildebrand said to look at it in the morning and make a note." Mia shrugged, a movement he caught out of the corner of his eye as he steered the car off of school grounds and onto the road back into River Hill. "I've never ridden a bus before."

Max winced. He'd known Isabel had put Mia in some kind of alternative school, but he hadn't been clear on what that actually meant. Unbidden, his memory flashed back to Lizzie Teague giving him an extremely dubious look when he'd announced that he'd master this fatherhood thing. He'd been too distracted by wanting to tear her clothes off to notice her distinct lack of confidence in him, but now it stung for some reason.

"We'll get the hang of this, Mia," he promised her as he passed the sign welcoming visitors to River Hill, population 10,940. "Want to come hang at the restaurant for a while?"

"Sure," she said, her voice small in the big cabin of his SUV.

He nodded, glad she'd agreed, since he was just now realizing that he didn't have a backup plan if she hadn't.

"I NEED HELP," Max hissed into the phone. "Stop laughing at me."

Jessica Casillas-Moore's chuckles faded, finally.

"I'm sorry, Max. I'm taking this whole thing very seriously, I promise."

"I can hear him laughing, too," Max said grimly. Sean Amory's howls in the background hadn't diminished in the slightest, even though his wife had managed to control herself.

"Sean," he heard Jess hiss. "He can hear you." She must have put her hand over the phone's microphone, because everything went a little muffled. All he heard was a yelp and a giggle, and then what might be a door closing, and finally, the voice of the head baker at The Breadery, the bakery across the square from Frankie's, was blessedly absent from his phone line.

"Doesn't he have apple fritters to fry, or something?" Max grumbled.

"No, he's back to Tuesdays for those," Jess said absently. "Look, how can I help you, exactly?"

Max sighed. "It turns out that nine year olds don't really do well with a restaurant schedule."

"I'm shocked." Her voice was dry.

"Your sister has kids, right? You helped out a lot with them?"

"Yes, my brothers and I all help out Marisol with the boys. Sean, too." Jess' voice took on a different note, one of pride mixed with anxiety, and Max winced. Sean and Jess had eloped at the beginning of the year, and her family hadn't been thrilled about it. Blending the Amorys with the Casillas-Moores was an ongoing challenge.

"So you know more about raising kids than I do."

"Max, a potato knows more about raising kids than you do."

Wow. His friends certainly didn't pull their punches. "Gee, thanks."

"So what is your plan, here? Are you calling me to ask for free babysitting? Because I'm sure your niece is nice and all, but my filming schedule is pretty intense right now." Jess was the host of a beauty and lifestyle show, a gig she'd scored due to the popularity of her blog and occasional segments on local morning news shows. She was increasingly in demand these days, something he knew because Sean obnoxiously brought it up every time they gathered for poker night. Sometimes—not that he'd ever admit it out loud— Max wondered what it would be like to be in a relationship like theirs. And then he remembered that he was almost never home, and relationships tended to rely on the people in them actually seeing each other. Which brought him back to his main issue.

"I mean, I wouldn't complain about babysitting," he said, just to annoy her. "But honestly, I think what Mia could really use is just... family, you know? You're good at family," he admitted grudgingly. "Probably the best I know."

There was silence on the other end of the line. "Well... thanks," she said. "Let me see what I can do about my schedule. And call Maeve, too."

"She's next on my list," Max said.

Ben's girlfriend came from a big Irish family, and she was one of the nicest people Max had ever known. She'd once drunkenly propositioned him with a marriage pact when she was regretting her singlehood, but then she'd met Ben. The two of them were made for each other, and Max hadn't worried at all about not taking Maeve up on the pact. She was far more like a sister to him than anything else. Red hair didn't do it for him, anyway. Not like blonde did.

And damn it, now he was thinking about Lizzie Teague again. The beautiful caseworker had been invading his brain for days now. He'd exchanged a few emails with her, keeping her up to date with the school registration process, and she was due for another home visit sometime next week. He didn't like how eager he was to see her again. After all, he was supposed to be doing what was right for Mia, not his dick. And no matter what that appendage thought about it, Lizzie was here for his niece. Not him. And if he couldn't keep it in his pants, she had the power to take Mia away. *Not going to happen.*

"All right. We'll work something out," Jess said. "Between all of us, I think we can figure out a way to keep you covered, Max."

"Thanks," he said, letting a little of the desperate gratitude he felt leak into his voice.

"You'd do the same for us," she pointed out. "Heck, you already have." It was the most direct reference she'd ever made to the fact that Max and Noah had once staged an intervention for Sean, who'd nearly succumbed to alcoholism when the demons of his past had been too much for him to handle.

He mumbled something about not mentioning it.

"Oh! I almost forgot—Angelica wants us all to get together. Did you see?"

"I think I saw a text come through, but I haven't really read it yet."

"How does brunch sound? Now that you're a dad, we might have to change our late night partying ways," Jess teased. "You'll bring Mia?"

"Will you make mole?" Max countered. Jess's grandmother's sauce recipe was one of the best things he'd ever tasted. Sean liked to say it was what had sealed the deal for him, even though they all knew he needed Jess like he needed air to breathe, mole or no.

"I could be persuaded."

THEY GATHERED at The Oakwell Inn, and Mia curled up into one of Angelica's plush couches immediately, drawing pad in hand. Max introduced her around, and she shyly greeted everyone. When it came to the last person to enter the room, Mia's eyes widened. "You're Naomi Klein?"

Naomi raised her elegant eyebrows. "You know me?"

"Your work," Mia blurted. Then she looked around

the room, realizing that she was the focus of everyone's attention, and turned bright red. "Never mind."

Iain Brennan, Naomi's partner, frowned thoughtfully at Mia, then turned to the rest of them. "I'm hungry," he announced. "Why is nobody in that beautiful kitchen back there?"

There was a brief silence, and then everyone filed obediently out of the room, chattering nonchalantly as though nothing had happened and they were all starving and in desperate need of mimosas. Which was probably true.

Max stayed behind, lounging in one of the upholstered chairs near the fireplace, as Naomi sat down on the couch next to Mia and somehow drew her into conversation now that the audience was gone.

"My mom's friend—" Mia glanced at Max, her expression as close to worried as he'd ever seen it. "Dave Murdoch. He showed me your work."

"Oh! I know Dave," Naomi said. "We worked together years ago." She frowned. "That's right, he's been spending time in Arizona at an artist's commune."

"My sister managed that commune," Max said.

He wondered if this Dave person was the rich boyfriend who'd recommended Isabel make a will. Naomi might like to pretend she was a starving artist, but she was quite popular in her own right, and she came from a high society family. She didn't pal around with nobodies. He made a mental note to ask Naomi more about the man in private, to make sure Isabel had been happy.

"Can I see your sketches?" Naomi asked.

Mia shyly agreed, and soon the two of them were leaning together on the couch, heads touching, talking a mile a minute about line technique and shading and pencil pressure and other things Max didn't understand.

Huh. Of all of his friends, Naomi was the last one he'd expected to get through to Mia. She'd developed a reputation as a little bit cold, a lot weird about her personal space, and deeply committed to never getting married or having children. But then again, she'd somehow wound up with Iain Brennan, who was a gentle, warm soul behind his beard and boxer's build. He was Maeve's older brother, after all. Kindness must run in the family.

His thoughts were interrupted by the return of most of his friends. Noah handed him a glass of champagne, and he frowned down at it, then up at his tall friend. "What's this for?" He got only an enigmatic smile in return, and he rolled his eyes.

"Does everyone have something?" Angelica asked. At the low chorus of assent, she beamed. "We have news."

Max waited, watching her. She had a glass of champagne herself, so she wasn't pregnant. Which must mean—

"We've picked a date for the wedding!" she exclaimed. "March fourteenth."

"Angelica, that's less than six months away," Maeve said, her Irish accent softly burring the words.

"I wouldn't want you all to get bored waiting for me," Angelica said, ignoring several snorts from the men in the room.

Noah had spent *years* trying to persuade Angelica to marry him, and then once she had agreed, finally getting her to commit to a date. He was a master at waiting for her, and they'd all heard about it quite a bit at poker nights and football games. He had her now, though, and he looked extremely smug about it. *Must be nice.*

Where had that stray thought come from? He banished it, just in time, because Angelica was turning to him like some sort of wedding-brained steamroller.

"Max, you'll cater, right?"

"Of course," he answered quickly. Then he glanced at Mia, who was shrinking into the couch, clearly attempting to be invisible. His schedule had just gotten even busier. And so had everyone else's. There went his help. Lizzie Teague was not going to be pleased.

4

———

*L*izzie tried not to pre-judge a situation. She knew better than most that when it came to raising a child who'd been thrust upon them without warning, sometimes uncles could resort to some pretty creative forms of child care. She'd worked the cash register at Uncle Horatio's antiques store more than once. Of course, that was only after her babysitter had broken both her arms in a lacrosse game a couple of hours before she was scheduled to come over. And then there was the time she'd joined Uncle Jonathan at his office for three days in a row when that same babysitter had gone to look at colleges while Uncle Horatio was in Paris scouring flea markets for his shop.

But both those times were the exception to the rule, and if the complaint that had been called into her office was to be believed, *this* was not. Max was incredibly lucky she had intercepted the message before her boss had. Hopefully, though, things weren't quite as dire as the concerned citizen had made it seem, and she could avert a disaster waiting to happen. She knew Max cared about Mia—and vice versa—so she was going to do her damnedest to prevent the girl from being placed in foster care.

But first, reconnaissance.

Lizzie checked her watch. If she'd timed her visit correctly, Max should be coming through the front door with Mia any second, and she'd be able to observe their interactions with one another undetected.

Like clockwork, the bell over the front door of the restaurant chimed, and the handsome chef and his sweet niece stepped inside, laughing at something Mia had just said. Lizzie's heart stuttered in her chest at seeing her appear so happy. After their heart-to-heart back at Max's house, she knew that more than anything Mia craved stability—a warm, loving environment where she could be a carefree, happy child instead of forever worrying about conforming to the ideas the leaders of the commune foisted on her.

During their hours-long discussion, Mia had

confessed she was afraid to start her period. A friend of hers at the commune had, and the subsequent chanting and dancing around a fire under the light of a full moon had frightened Mia terribly. Not that Lizzie could blame her. Starting your period was scary enough; being forced to celebrate it in such a way had Lizzie thanking her lucky stars that her uncles had had a much more practical approach to the subject. Namely, taking her to the family doctor and having the kind old nurse there explain everything to all of them.

Lizzie smiled fondly, recalling the look of horror on Jonathan and Horatio's faces as Nurse Taylor had described, in explicit and excruciating detail, exactly what happened to a woman's body each month. By some failure of education—or possibly willful ignorance—neither of the two middle-aged men had known it was a regular occurrence that lasted decades.

That was probably something she should also mention to Max, though she had a sneaking suspicion he knew a bit more about women than her gay uncles. Assuming, of course, he retained custody of his niece. At that thought, her stomach pitched with anxiety, and she told herself it was the same reaction she'd have for any family. After all, her job was to keep them together, not tear them apart. Her concern for the handsome man on the other side of the room had nothing to do with the fact that she had been fantasizing about what he looked like naked.

Across the way, Max ruffled Mia's hair affection-ately as she settled into a booth, shyly lifting her hand in greeting to one of the servers waiting tables in that section of the restaurant. Lizzie continued to watch as Max departed through a swinging double door, leaving his niece unattended. A few seconds later Mia and the server exchanged some verbal pleasantries—she couldn't hear what was being said from where she sat —and then the girl smiled and nodded as she reached into her backpack and pulled out a folder and several sheafs of paper.

Not too long after, the server dropped off a pink, bubbly drink and a plate of what looked to be hummus and pita chips. The next hour followed a similar pattern. Every ten minutes or so one of Max's employees would stop by Mia's table, share a few words with her, and then go back to work. Every so often, someone would spend a couple of minutes with her, checking over what Lizzie assumed was her homework.

Sometime during the second hour of her observation, a tall, willowy brunette entered the restaurant with a large rectangular satchel swinging against her hip, making a bee-line directly for Mia's table. Her hair —while pulled into an elegant bun—was caked liberally with mud, and her clothes were splattered with paint.

Lizzie sat up in her seat, ready to act. Mia had told her that most of the artists who spent time at the commune had begrudgingly tolerated her presence, but one of its full-time residents had been kind, looking after her when Isabel was otherwise occupied. Lizzie had no reason to think the woman had driven from Arizona to California to try to take Mia back there, but her senses were on red alert anyhow. She'd heard—and seen—worse in her line of work, and as sad as it was, she didn't trust anyone she hadn't personally vetted.

It turned out she needn't have worried. Mia smiled and gathered her homework up into in a neat pile and then pushed it all to the side. As the woman slid into the booth, Mia pulled a notebook and a set of pencils from her backpack and set them out on the table. Lizzie watched as the woman pulled her own supplies out of the satchel and arranged them alongside Mia's. She notched her head toward Mia's work and said something that made the girl blush before picking up a pencil and adding a few strokes of her own to the paper. When she was finished, Mia's head shot up, then back down to the paper, and up again, her face split in a wide grin.

"That's my friend Naomi," came an amused voice from directly behind Lizzie.

She jumped in her seat, turning to find Max staring down at her, his hands planted on his trim waist and his lips quirked to the side in a wry grin.

"Oh, hi. Umm ..." Flustered at being caught spying, Lizzie sputtered out a few nonsensical words and then took a deep breath before starting over. "Hello, Mr. Vergaras."

"I thought we agreed that you would call me Max." He grabbed the back of the chair across from her, showing off a dusting of dark hair over tan skin peeking out from beneath the rolled up sleeves of his red checked flannel shirt. Without invitation, he pulled it out and dropped down into it, linking his fingers together on the tabletop between them. "Or are we back to using formalities?"

Lizzie forced herself to look up from those strong, masculine hands, hating herself for noticing the jagged scar that bisected his right thumb and wondering how he'd gotten it. A knife cut, no doubt. And why did the image of Max's full lips wrapped around his thumb turn her on so much? Unfortunately, looking at his face was no better, since now she was staring into eyes the color of the whiskey sauce of her favorite toffee cake.

And now she was hungry *and* horny. Horngry.

Suddenly, she was conscious of how empty she was, both her belly and her—*No!* she thought with silent rebuke. *Must not think of all the things I'd like to have filled by this man.*

She felt her face go scarlet, but fought to otherwise control her features by taking a deep breath and blowing it out as she counted down from five.

There, that's better.

"Unfortunately, I'm here on a *formal* visit. We received a report from—"

"Margaret Marsh?" His eyes flashed with barely leashed anger as he practically spat the woman's name.

He was right, of course, but Lizzie couldn't tell him so. "I'm sorry, but I'm not at liberty to reveal where the complaint originated, only that we take them very seriously."

His jaw ticked and he looked away briefly. After a few seconds, his chest lifted and he blew a breath out through his nose before bringing his face back around. His eyes flicked down to the manila folder sitting next to her bread plate. "Let me guess. You're here investigating me for abuse."

From his tone, she got the impression Mrs. Marsh had already expressed her concerns to Max, who'd either chosen to ignore her, or had had words with her about it. "Not abuse so much as neglect," she clarified as stoically and dispassionately as she could.

Max crossed his arms over his chest and stared her down. "That's bullshit, and you know it."

She *did* know it.

The last few weeks, they'd exchanged several emails, mostly Max asking for her advice on how to make Mia feel welcome in her new home, but sometimes they'd also shared funny memes they'd come across. After she'd sent one of a mother orangutan working tirelessly to corral her baby, Max had confessed that it had come at the best possible time. He'd already driven to and from St. Aloysius twice that day with forgotten school supplies and finished homework, and he'd just discovered that Mia had left her lunchbox in the back of his Land Rover so he was on his way back there. In response, she'd sent him a "hang in there" cat meme, telling him that it got easier.

And it would. Eventually.

But in the meantime, she had to make sure his niece wasn't taken away from him.

Which meant he needed to arrange for a real babysitter. What if the restaurant was busy and the servers couldn't chat with her as they went about their duties? Mia didn't seem like the type of kid to sneak off when no one was looking, but she *was* a kid. They didn't often do what you expected, or what was in their best interest.

And as they'd already established, Mia had grown up as free range as they came. While it seemed out of character, it wouldn't be a *complete* shock to Lizzie if Mia *did* get up and wander off when she got tired of waiting on her uncle to close down the restaurant for the night.

"While it's my professional opinion there's no reason for CPS to get involved, you *have* to get a babysitter, Max," she told him.

He opened his mouth to interrupt—likely to offer up an excuse for why he'd been unable to arrange for one yet—but she held up her hand to waylay his rebuttal. "A *real* babysitter. Your staff seem perfectly nice, and Mia appears awfully fond of both them and your friend Naomi, but the restaurant can be loud and chaotic. What if she had slipped out when no one was paying attention?"

He uncrossed his arms and settled his forearms on the table, his fingers clenched into tight fists in front of her. "I *had* a babysitter. A high schooler from my neighborhood. She quit when her boyfriend complained she wasn't spending enough time with him. Incidentally, the guy's nineteen. Maybe you should look into him instead."

The hair on the back of Lizzie's neck prickled with remembered shame. Once upon a time, she'd been a young, impressionable teen who'd fallen prey to an older guy. Only, he hadn't stuck around long enough to demand more of her time. Just the opposite, in fact. Once she'd given him her virginity, he'd bailed, admitting that he had a girlfriend back in college.

She pushed the memory of that painful summer to the back of her mind and steeled her shoulders. "I will if you think I need to. Eighteen is the age of consent in California."

He waved his hand in front of his face, looking slightly embarrassed. "No, don't bother. Pedro's actually a good kid. He's leaving for the Marines in a couple of months, so of course he wants to spend time with his girl. And she's of age, or within days of it, I think. Her parents love him. I'm just being selfish because that means I don't have a babysitter on Wednesday nights."

"Just Wednesdays?" she asked, wondering why that incredibly important piece of information had been excluded from Mrs. Marsh's complaint. From the report, Lizzie had been led to believe that Mia was left to her own devices on a nightly basis, but given that tonight was Wednesday, it made sense that she was here today.

Max nodded, and shoved his hand through his hair, tugging at the roots. "I've called literally everyone I know, and no one can do Wednesdays."

Lizzie fidgeted with the straw in her iced tea as an idea began to take shape.

Don't you dare say it, a voice at the back of her head warned even as as the rest of her brain hurtled toward a decision. With a deep breath, she willed the butterflies in her stomach to settle down. If they didn't, she might literally be sick. She was about to step over a *huge* line, but it was one she thought she could justify if push came to shove. Technically, what she did in her off hours was her own business, as long as it wasn't illegal. Not to mention, she was Mia's caseworker, and therefore she was at least partially responsible for making sure the girl had the best possible care.

She pushed the air out of her lungs slowly, flattened her palms on the table, and raised her eyes to Max's. "You didn't call me."

5

He wasn't going to take Lizzie up on her offer. He couldn't, could he? Wasn't her getting involved like this some kind of conflict of interest?

And even if it wasn't for her, it sure as hell was for him. He didn't know if he could handle Lizzie in his house more than she was for professional purposes. He was already spending every night dreaming about her, waking up hard and jerking off in the shower with thoughts of how those luscious lips would feel on him, how *she* would feel on him ... around him.

But also, he was desperate.

In response to her statement, he managed to mumble something non-committal, not missing the sharp-eyed glance she gave him. Lizzie Teague wasn't stupid. If he wasn't jumping to accept the offer like a man jumping out of a river, there was a reason for it. And the heat in her eyes when she looked at him suggested that she knew what it was just as well as he did.

And yet, she'd offered anyway.

Oh, god. How had his life become so complicated?

He pasted on a smile and led her over to where Mia and Naomi were playing the sketch game they'd invented, letting her sit down with them so they could explain it to her and she could subtly interrogate Mia, something Naomi understood judging by the frown she gave him. He shrugged at her before escaping back to the kitchen, looking for something he could chop, sear, or toss to distract himself from thinking about all the things he wanted to do to his niece's caseworker.

Of course Wendy, the chef he'd hired a few years ago, had everything well in hand. She didn't need his help; frankly, he needed her a lot more than she needed him, so he usually tried to stay out of her way. Hell, most of the time he wanted to kiss the ground she walked on. They had a great working relationship that was vital to the success of Frankie's.

As the owner, he developed the recipes and menus while she did the cooking. Most of his time was spent paying bills, answering emails, and submitting maintenance requests for equipment. He loved being a chef, but that was because he liked to make interesting food. He enjoyed seeing his friends and loved ones' eyes light up when they tasted something he'd created. Which was why these days, he spent time out front as often as he could. Occasionally, he even found time to retreat to the kitchen when he felt the need to touch ingredients, to remind himself what it was like to be back there.

Or, you know, escape from sexy caseworkers he shouldn't be thinking about in that way.

Wendy rolled her eyes at him when he asked what he could do, and in her usual profanity-laden tone informed him that he was in the way. She hip-checked him as he passed, and he growled at her, then found his way over to an empty prep station with a checklist above it. He julienned vegetables until he could think straight, and by the time he came out of the kitchen, dinnertime guests were trickling in and Lizzie was gone.

Thank god. Now he didn't have to answer her about the babysitting.

Two days later, he was wishing he had. Friday's prep had been interrupted by a phone call from the school again. He thought they'd been doing so well, too, making it to November without any more calls. It had seemed like they were falling into a routine. Mia was her quiet, contained self, sliding seamlessly into his life with as little disruption possible. And when he *did* need help, his friends were there for him. He had everything under control.

But this was as far from under control as it got. Currently, he stood in the office at St. Aloysius, watching helplessly as Mia sobbed hysterically into the ample chest of Sheryl the Office Lady.

"She's been like this since before school ended," a voice murmured from behind him. He turned to see Mia's teacher, Mrs. Hildebrand. "I sent her down here in the hopes that she might be able to calm down, but I don't think it's working. And she didn't even try to get on the bus."

"What happened?" he asked.

She sighed. "Honestly, Mr. Vergaras, I don't know. Girls can be mean to each other at this age, but I didn't think Mia was having any trouble with her classmates. There wasn't a specific incident that I saw. She just ... she's having a hard time." The teacher's eyes were troubled as she looked at Mia.

Max cursed himself inwardly. He hadn't noticed. Or he had, and he'd thought Mia was just ... handling it. But obviously he was an idiot. Nine year old girls didn't simply *handle* the sudden deaths of their mothers and the subsequent upheaval of their entire lives.

He moved forward and worked with Sheryl to transfer Mia's clinging body to himself. She didn't seem to notice the hand-off through her sobbing, but when he had her in his arms she buried her head in his neck.

He coughed under the pressure, breathed a quiet "thank you" to the women, and carried his niece to the car. Eventually, on the long ride home, her sobs stopped, but her stuttery, panicked breathing didn't. Neither did the endless tears running down her face. And if all of that wasn't bad enough, she wouldn't speak to him at all.

He pulled into the driveway after exhausting every possible attempt at conversation he could think of, and fired off a text to Wendy to let her know he wasn't coming back for the dinner rush. She sent him a shrug emoji in return.

Nice to be needed, he thought, shoving his phone back down into the front pocket of his jeans.

And speaking of needed—Mia clearly *needed* more than just him. Or rather, more than what he knew how to do or give her. He was in over his head. Maybe if he'd known Mia her entire life, been her *actual* parent instead of just this shitty substitute, he'd know what to do here. Or maybe not. Either way, he needed help. He ran through his options in his head, grimacing as he carried Mia into the house, her tears drenching his shoulder.

Naomi, as good as she was with Mia, wasn't going to be able to help here. Ice Queen Klein didn't really do emotions as far as Max could tell. Angelica was too overbearing—he adored Noah's fiancée, but she was quintessentially A Lot. Maeve and Ben were in San Francisco for the weekend to watch her favorite rugby team play, and Jess was at some beauty products convention. And even if they were all in town, the truth was, none of his friends really knew kids that well either, particularly not girls. Maeve and Jess both had nephews—not nieces—and none of them had gone through much trauma, thank goodness.

There was exactly one person in his contacts list who would know what to do here.

With shaking hands, he typed out a quick message. He would probably regret this later, but he'd deal with that when the time came. Right now was about addressing Mia's needs.

Max: SOS. I need your help. It's Mia.

He didn't have to wait long for the reply to come.

Lizzie: I'll be there in ten.

She made it in nine, and when he opened the door for her, Max almost swallowed his tongue. As it was, he was pretty sure his jaw was somewhere on the floor.

"Sorry," she said. "I was at the gym."

That much was obvious. He'd only ever seen her in work clothes before—well-tailored, professional outfits that flowed gently around her curves. And yet, as unsexy as they were probably intended to be, he'd wanted to strip her out of them. But Lizzie standing before him in gym clothes? He was pretty sure his brain had completely stopped functioning. The one on top of his neck, anyway.

"What is it? What happened?" she asked urgently, eyes dark with worry as he stood there like a statue, momentarily too stunned to speak. She hefted the black and pink duffel bag she was carrying up onto her shoulder. "I've got a first aid kit, menstrual supplies, snacks, and the numbers for five different pediatricians."

Finally finding his voice, he stepped back and allowed her to enter the house. "You gathered all that in ten minutes?"

She shook her head as she pressed past him. "I keep it in my car."

He closed the door, swallowing down the rush of heat that had flashed through his entire body when she'd made contact on her way inside. Now was emphatically not the time.

"Mia?" she called.

"She's on the couch," he said, but Lizzie was already there, and Mia had virtually leapt into her arms, the sobbing starting anew.

Lizzie lifted a startled gaze to him, and he raised his hands helplessly. "I haven't been able to find out—"

"My mom is de-he-he-he-heaaaaad!" Mia wailed.

Fuck. He'd really screwed this up. Max closed his eyes and his body went limp. He slouched against the wall and watched as Lizzie, with gentle touches and quiet murmurs, somehow calmed Mia down. She had to be some kind of wizard. It was the only explanation.

Finally, he found the courage to join them on the couch. He sat on the other side of his niece and tried to ignore the little voice in his head that was shouting *this is what a family feels like*.

Lizzie looked over Mia's head at him. "The school is hosting a mother-daughter spa day fundraiser," she said quietly.

"Fuck," he blurted.

Mia raised her head. "Uncle Max."

"Sorry. Sorry," he said to Lizzie. "I'm trying."

Her lips thinned in what looked like an unwilling smile. "I know you are."

He sighed, and wrapped an arm around Mia, letting his hand rest against Lizzie's shoulder. He told himself there was nowhere else for it to go. "What can I do, Mia?"

She shook her head, once more pillowed against Lizzie's chest. "Nothing."

"Want to play hooky from school that day?"

Mia nodded.

Realizing how that might have sounded, he winced, and glanced back up at Lizzie. "Pretend you didn't hear that."

Now her smile was real. "Hear what?"

Damn. That smile. It did things to him. Things that he didn't want to think about right now. He needed to focus on Mia, not the light flush that rose in Lizzie's cheeks the longer he continued to stare at her.

Eventually, she blinked, breaking their connection.

"How does a quick dinner sound?" he asked. "Pasta?"

"Not hungry," Mia mumbled.

"Here," Lizzie said, digging behind her in her bag. "Eat this protein bar and I'll take you up to bed. Sound good?"

Mia yawned and nodded, reaching for the wrapped bar.

Max raised an eyebrow at Lizzie, and she shrugged. "Something's better than nothing."

He let Lizzie take Mia upstairs, frowning after her as she went, wondering how often those protein bars served as breakfast, lunch, and dinner combined. He might not be able to jump her bones, but like hell was he going to let her subsist on squirrel food. Shaking his head, he made his way to the kitchen to do what he did best. Well, second best.

Stop that, he chided himself.

When Lizzie came back downstairs, he had the pasta boiling. He pointed to one of the chairs at the table. "Sit." She sat. "Please tell me you weren't planning on eating a protein bar for dinner."

She chuckled. "It's not a regular habit of mine, but sometimes I snag one after my workout on Fridays."

"Well, I'm making you dinner whether you like it or not." He slung eggs and cream into a bowl, and chopped some thick cut bacon into lardons as he spoke. "And thanks for coming over. I, uh, didn't know what to do."

She sighed. "I wouldn't expect you to."

"Ouch."

"No, I don't mean—" she protested.

"No, I get it." He shrugged and grabbed the pasta strainer. "I was thinking the same thing when I texted you. I'm not—" he swallowed past the lump in his throat. "I'm not really Mia's parent."

"Oh, Max." Lizzie rose and came to stand next to him at the stove as the bacon sizzled away. "You're doing a great job. This is a really hard thing to ask of anybody." She smiled briefly. "I've been the girl having the breakdown, and I've been the person on the other side, too."

"Is Mia going to be okay? What can I do for her?" He slid the bacon over the drained pasta, then lashed the whole thing with the mixture of eggs and cream, reaching into his spice cabinet for nutmeg with his other hand. "Grab a plate, that cabinet over there."

"To be blunt, therapy." Lizzie reached up and pulled down two plates, and he resolutely ignored the way it made her tank top stretch over those enticing curves.

"You sound like my friend Noah. He dealt with some of his issues with therapy, and now he thinks everyone needs it."

She laughed. "He's not wrong. Honestly, most

people could use at least a little bit of therapy. It's a healthy choice, you know?"

"Do you have anyone you recommend? For Mia," he added quickly.

She shot him a shrewd glance. Of course she noticed the hasty qualification. "Yes. I'll email you a list with my comments as soon as I'm at a computer, if that works."

He nodded. Everybody needed therapy, huh? Well, it might be true, but if he was going to see a therapist about his conflicted feelings about Isabel, and parenthood, and who knows what else, he'd find one on his own.

He dished out two servings of pasta, twisting his wrist as he laid it on the plate so that the strands landed in a neat little nest. Just because he was cooking at home didn't mean his food shouldn't be pretty. Angelica laughed whenever he told her that in their sporadic cooking lessons, but he'd seen her serve up some lovely dishes at the dinner parties she liked to host at The Oakwell these days.

"Here you go. Sit. Eat." He pointed Lizzie firmly back toward the table.

"I'm sitting, I'm eating!" she laughed as she fell into her seat. "Oh, my god, Max." Her eyes nearly rolled backward in her head as she took her first bite. "This is incredible."

Smiling, he watched her shove the fork back into her mouth. This was why he loved to cook. It made people *happy*. And making Lizzie happy was ... well, he wanted to do it again. And again, and again.

Didn't I tell you to stop? his conscience groused.

Before he could find himself planning out all the dishes he wanted to cook for her, he changed the subject.

"If it's not too much trouble, I think I'll take you up on that Wednesday babysitting," he said.

She grinned up at him, and sirens began blaring in his head as his brain fired off all of Lizzie's greatest attributes . *Great with Mia. Smart. Funny. Incredibly hot. This woman should be MINE.*

He ignored it all. Surely he could get through the next few months without jumping on Lizzie like a crazed, sex-starved animal. The custody declaration would be finalized shortly after Angelica's wedding. He just had to get through—quickly, he tallied the days in his head—the holidays. *Oh, god.* He was so screwed.

6

S nap. "Hello, Earth to Elizabeth."

With a blink, Lizzie's eyes focused in on Kate Zomer. Her boss was not happy.

"I'm sorry; what?" Lost in her daydreams about a certain sexy Argentinian chef, she'd forgotten Kate was even standing there. In an effort to pretend she'd been working and not staring off into space wondering what Max's lightly stubbled jaw would taste like if she licked it, she clacked her fingers against the keyboard of her laptop.

The night she'd rushed to his house to console a distraught Mia, it had taken everything in her willpower not to launch herself out of her seat and lick off a drop of pasta sauce his napkin had missed while they'd eaten dinner together.

"Did you hear a word I said?" Kate crossed her arms over her chest and tapped the toe of her shoe against the scuffed linoleum.

Lizzie wracked her brain to try and piece the threads of the conversation together. The last thing she recalled hearing was something about mileage and expense reports.

Aha! That was it.

"Oh, I absolutely agree," she answered, hoping to appease her persnickety boss. "You're right; it's no wonder caseworkers are quitting left and right. What's next? We'll have to buy our own computers?" Honestly, Lizzie wouldn't be surprised if that was the next money-saving measure the county tried to impose on them. With the cost of gas nearing five dollars a gallon in the Bay Area due to the state-wide mandate that refineries produce cleaner gas with fewer emissions, her boss's bosses in Sacramento were finding new and inventive ways to pinch pennies.

Kate's eyes narrowed as she bent forward to inspect Lizzie's face more closely. "Are you on drugs, Elizabeth?"

"What? No!" Lizzie pushed back from her desk, causing her chair to roll backward and crash into the bookshelf behind her with a *thud*. "Why would you think that?"

"You've been distracted for *weeks*, and every time I've walked past your desk today, you're staring off in a stupor. I know marijuana is legal in California, but let me remind you—"

"I assure you, I am *not* on drugs," Lizzie blurted before her boss could threaten to fire her for something she hadn't done. *Ever.* "I've just …" She blew out a breath and ran a hand through her hair. "I've just had a lot on my mind is all," she finished lamely.

Kate let out an unsatisfied sounding *harrumph*. "If you say so."

She nodded. "I *do* say so. I've never done drugs."

At the next desk over, her co-worker Maggie chuckled under her breath and muttered something that sounded suspiciously like, "You really don't know what you're missing."

"What was that, Margaret?" Kate barked as she turned to face her other employee.

Maggie glanced up from her computer, her eyes wide with feigned ignorance. "I didn't say anything."

"I heard you mumble something." Kate's accusatory glare bounced between Maggie and Lizzie, her dark burgundy lips flattened into a scowl and her bushy eyebrows pinched into a frown.

Lizzie generally tried not to think unkindly about other women, but with her tight perm and exaggerated makeup, Kate Zomer could double as a character in a movie or TV show set in the eighties. The outdated clothes she wore simply added to the overall effect.

Supposedly, she was only forty-five, but she looked and acted like a woman approaching her sixties. Her sartorial choices baffled Lizzie. And her management style left a lot to be desired. Unwieldy mileage reports weren't the only thing that had caused several of her coworkers to leave.

"Sorry," Maggie said with a lift of her shoulders as her gaze dropped back down to her computer. "Wasn't me."

Kate stared at Maggie for a few protracted seconds before eventually turning her attention back to Lizzie, ruby-clawed finger pointed at her for emphasis. "I expect to have those reports on my desk by tomorrow morning."

Lizzie gulped. What reports? Her eyes quickly darted to her computer to scan her inbox for an email she might have missed. Unfortunately, there was nothing there about a report she was supposed to be working on. She swallowed again. *Shit*. There really was no excuse for not knowing what Kate was talking about. There was a man-sized hole in her memory, and the blame fell squarely on her inappropriate fascination with Max Vergaras.

Actually, this thing with him had passed the 'fascination' phase several weeks ago, morphing into a full-blown obsession. One she *really* needed to nip in the bud.

Except … that wasn't necessarily easy, since she saw him every Wednesday when she babysat Mia. *Which you volunteered to do*, her conscience reminded her helpfully. And sure, her lustful thoughts probably weren't helped by the way her pulse spiked when he walked in the door late at night and greeted her in a low, gravelly whisper lest he wake his young ward sleeping upstairs.

And then there were the near-daily text messages to one another. Lizzie was ashamed to admit it, but they'd turned a little flirty lately. Although, now that she thought about it, Max *was* a chef. Maybe yesterday he really had been talking about an actual sausage and not his—*NO*, she thought, pushing that dirty image aside. They'd never stepped over the lines of impropriety, and they never could.

But that didn't mean she hadn't fantasized about it … oh, just about a million and one times. Especially at night. When she was naked.

And now she was craving sausage for dinner.

"Elizabeth?" Kate pressed, breaking into her wayward thoughts.

Again.

"Um, yes. The report …" she trailed off, wondering if she should just admit that she had no earthly idea what her boss was talking about.

"—I'm just double checking the numbers now," Maggie interjected with a wink in Lizzie's direction. "We'll have it on your desk by noon tomorrow."

"I said I need it in the morning," Kate snapped.

Maggie slid her chair back from her desk and

crossed her arms over her chest as she lifted her right eyebrow high. "And *I* said you'd have it by lunch time. You can't dump something like this on us at the end of the day and expect to have it back by the morning. Especially when you've known about this meeting for three weeks."

Ah, *that* report. She, Maggie, and another case-worker named Lorenzo had been piloting a new program for at-risk teens, and were due to share their findings with the department brass on Monday. Or rather, Kate was. *They'd* done all the work, but now their boss was going to get the credit for it.

Lizzie breathed out a frustrated sigh as she double-clicked on a folder on her desktop. *Oh well,* she thought, as the spreadsheet filled her screen. *No use dwelling on it.* Unless she was willing to peruse the job listings Maggie forwarded her every Monday, this was just how it was going to be, she reminded herself as she pulled all the information together for Maggie and uploaded it to their shared drive. She rubbed her temples and started counting down the minutes until she could leave.

LIZZIE LOOKED up from the book she was reading as the front door crept slowly open and Max made his way inside the house.

"Sorry I'm late," he whispered, toeing off his shoes

and hanging his jacket next to hers on the hooks lining the wall in his foyer. "One of the steam wells sprung a leak and it took me forever to find it. Couldn't get a rep from the company out during a weeknight dinner rush either, so I had to learn some emergency plumbing. Thank god for YouTube." He rolled his eyes.

Her gaze flicked to the wooden clock hanging over the fireplace to check the time, and then she set her book to the side and stretched her arms into the air, her back popping with relief. "No worries, I've just been catching up on some reading. Mia's been asleep for a couple of hours." She pushed to her feet, the quick upward motion causing a stab of pain directly in the center of her forehead. She screwed her eyes shut and pinched the bridge of her nose in an effort to quell the nausea that accompanied her worsening headache.

When the pounding abated, she opened her eyes to find Max standing directly in front of her, worry written on his face. "Are you okay?" He reached out to cup her forearm in his large, warm palm.

She nodded, the motion making her slightly dizzy. "Yeah, just a migraine I've been fighting since this afternoon."

He led her back to the sofa and gently eased her down onto its cushions. "You should have said something when you picked Mia up. I could have found someone else to watch her if you're not feeling well." She cast him a dubious look. "Okay, you're right. I couldn't have. But one night at the restaurant isn't going to kill her. We've done it before."

"It's eleven o'clock, Max. Her bedtime is eight, and she needs her sleep. She has that big geography test tomorrow."

"Shit. I could have sworn that was on Friday." He sighed and ran his hand through his hair, causing the thick, wavy strands to stick up at odd angles. This close, she could see his hair was generally in a shambles. He must have been doing that all night. "I thought I was getting better at keeping her schedule straight."

Without conscious thought, she set her hand on his knee and squeezed. "It's okay. I quizzed her before she took her shower and she's going to rock it. That kid knows her state capitols better than most adults."

Max's eyes darted down to where Lizzie's hand rested, and then back up, his pupils dilated. "You're amazing, you know that?"

A comforting warmth settled over her, and with it, her headache lessened. It'd been so long since a man had looked at her that way that she'd almost forgotten what it felt like. She'd been so careful around Max these past few weeks, but with her defenses low from the tough day at work and her ensuing headache, she allowed herself a quiet moment to bask in his overt appreciation.

"Thank you," she said, sliding her hand from his knee and linking her fingers in her lap. "But Mia's the amazing one. And I know you sometimes question yourself, but she's lucky to have you. She's really thriving."

His eyes locked onto hers for several long seconds. In the distance, Lizzie could hear the ticking of the clock, but her attention was fixed on the handsome man sitting next to her, the heat of his body mingling with her own. She knew she should look away—*move* away—but his gaze was hypnotic, his proximity magnetic. Those dark amber irises held her firmly in his thrall as he murmured, "And who takes care of you?"

At his insinuation, her heart clanged against her breastbone, a runaway train heading straight for disaster. One she needed to stave off if she knew what was good for them. "Max ..." she whispered, even as her body swayed toward him. "We can't."

His tongue darted out to lick a quick path over his lush bottom lip. "I know," he said. "Trust me; I know. But you feel it too, right? I'm not just imagining this."

She shook her head slowly back and forth as his palm found her waist, the heat of his touch nearly burning her to ash. "You're not imagining it. I feel it too. So, so much." Her voice broke on that last word. It had been two years since she'd been touched by a man, and her body craved the connection like it craved its next breath. His fingers inching their way up her spine were everything she needed ... and everything she couldn't have. Abruptly, she scooted out of his grasp. "If we'd met under different circumstances …"

He moved back then too, clearing his throat as he went. "Right. Of course. What was I thinking?" His face dropped forward and he stared at the rug at his feet, visibly guilty.

Lizzie knew how hard he'd taken Isabel's death, and all the ways he still struggled with stepping into the role of parent for Mia. For weeks, she'd watched him devote everything he had to raising his sweet niece, and he took every tiny setback personally. More than once, in their quiet conversations after Mia had gone to bed, he'd confessed to feeling like a complete and utter failure—a notion she'd been quick to try and dispel. But the defeated look on his face right now was the same one she'd seen when he'd told her he worried he was doing more harm than good.

And so, despite the warning bells sounding in her head, she stood and moved closer, setting her hand on his shoulder. His head sprung up, his eyes searching hers, begging for … something she couldn't name. Or rather, something she *could* name, but knew it was wiser not to.

"You were thinking … " she trailed off. She knew what she *wanted* to say, but knew just as well these feelings had her walking a professional tightrope with no safety net below her. If she messed up and did something that could jeopardize her career—or worse, the stability this small family unit had managed to carve out for themselves in the face of tragedy—she'd never forgive herself.

So rather than giving voice to the words in her heart, she let her unfinished sentence lie. Instead, she said, "You're doing a great job with Mia. Truly. It's late, and we just got carried away. It happens." It didn't—not ever—but it felt like the right thing to say in the moment, a way to let him off the hook for his guilt.

For several long seconds he gazed up at her, his face flashing through a bevy of emotions: confusion, understanding, frustration, and then acceptance. "I know what you're doing, Lizzie."

"You do?" She swallowed deeply. Hell, *she* barely knew what she was doing.

"I do. And I appreciate it." He leaned back against the cushions, his body suddenly sapped of energy as his palms rested on either side of his thighs.

Lizzie stared down at him, giving herself a torturous minute to imagine taking a step forward, placing her knees on the couch, and then straddling his strong, tired body. A quick moment to imagine putting her palms to his cheek and kissing away all his doubt and worry. A brief second to imagine him wrapping his arms around her waist and taking control of the kiss, laying her out on the couch and taking control of ... everything.

But that was all it could be between them. Imaginary. So instead she took a step backward, and then another, and another until she was in the foyer reaching for her coat and purse. "Goodnight, Max," she said as she pulled open the door and walked out into the chilly November night.

"Goodbye," she whispered again as she pulled her car down the long drive and into the darkness of wine country at midnight.

*L*izzie wasn't answering his texts. Max had held off a few days, trying to give them both some space. But he couldn't resist for long, so he'd texted her about Mia's latest homework project. Unfortunately, she hadn't answered.

Nor had she responded to the one about his latest menu addition—a kale salad with a pear vinaigrette. She'd once mentioned pears were her favorite fruit. And he was in way over his head if he was adding all her favorites to his menu, but he'd texted her about it anyway.

He'd also called her office line during the day, but her voice mail message had informed him she was out of the office, which didn't surprise him. With the number of home visits she did for her clients, she was out more often than she was in. Her cell went straight to voicemail, too. He left a couple of casual messages, as though he were just checking in with her about Mia, all the while trying to ignore the tension ratcheting through his body.

Had he really screwed things up that badly? She wanted him as much as he wanted her; she'd as much as said so. But they both knew they couldn't act on it—not in the position they were in.

His mind drifted to the future. What if she weren't Mia's caseworker anymore? What if the guardianship were finalized, and there was nothing more between them than this incredible attraction?

It wasn't just attraction, though.

Lizzie Teague was somehow everything he wanted in his life. He'd once told Maeve he didn't particularly like being single, but dating wasn't something that had been on his radar lately either. Frankie's kept him plenty busy. And his inbox had been blowing up lately —there was serious investor interest in franchising his restaurant, and he didn't know if he wanted to or not. Opening up another Frankie's seemed like it would diminish what made the original one so special, the love and care he'd lavished on it to make it his dream restaurant. But now that he had more than himself to worry about, maybe the extra income would be useful? Mia was only nine, but he realized he should probably start thinking about college funds for her.

With a quirk of his lips, he tucked his niece's lunch into her backpack, wondering if this was what parents felt like when they decided to have a second child. Frankie's was his first baby; did he have enough room in his heart for more restaurants?

"Last day before Thanksgiving, kiddo," he said. "You excited?"

She nodded enthusiastically. "I love not going to school."

He frowned. "Is everything okay there?" After her meltdown a few weeks ago, he'd scheduled weekly appointments for her with the therapist Lizzie had recommended, and she'd finally started opening up. Nothing was going to make her an extrovert like Isabel had been, but he was keeping his eyes peeled for anything that might cause a setback.

She rolled her eyes at him. "Everything's fine, Uncle Max. Every kid likes not going to school."

"That's probably true. I don't know a lot of kids, but I was one once, you know."

"Yeah, right."

"I was! Younger than you, even."

Mia shook her head, laughter in her eyes. "I don't think so. I think you just showed up one day as a grown-up chef."

"Um, and miss out on all the fun kid stuff? No

thank you." He nudged her toward the door. "Bus is coming."

She gave him a quick hug and darted down the driveway, waving hello to Mr. Becker, the bus driver, as she climbed aboard. He closed the door, returning to the kitchen to clean up their breakfast dishes.

After he finished loading the dishwasher, he found himself staring blankly at his phone, willing Lizzie to text him back. It buzzed once, causing him to jump, but it was just a supplier notifying him that his shipment of bok choy was ready. He set the device screen-down on the countertop and shoved his hands deep into his pockets. He stared at his phone for a beat, telling himself to leave it alone. He couldn't, though. Giving in to the impulse to reach out to her one last time, he sighed and picked it up, dialing her number.

Instead of going directly to voicemail like it had been, it actually rang this time, and he was so surprised he nearly dropped the phone into the sink.

"Hi, Max," she said.

"Hi." He stopped. He hadn't actually planned any further than this, especially given that she hadn't been answering him for most of a week.

"Is everything okay?"

He cleared his throat. "Uh, yeah."

"I got your messages. I'm sorry, my phone was off."

"Oh. Uh, good. I mean, okay." He winced. Could this conversation be any more awkward? Then inspiration struck. Why hadn't he thought of it before? "Listen, I wanted to ask—I mean, I guess it's a little short notice, but are you doing anything for Thanksgiving?" She didn't have family in town, he knew. "We always do a little Friendsgiving thing at the restaurant, just our group of friends and anyone we know who wants a place to go for the holiday. Mia's really excited..." he trailed off, realizing the fact that he was willing to use his niece as a bribe was... probably not admirable. He didn't quite care, though.

There was a pause on the other end of the line. "I'm sorry," she started.

"It's not—I mean, not because of us," he blurted. "Not that there's an *us*. I know we can't. I just thought you might—"

"—I appreciate the offer," she interjected. "But I'm actually out of town at my uncles' place for the weekend already."

"Ah. Oh."

"That's why my phone was off. I drove up here and left it in my bag. So my boss wouldn't call me, honestly." The ripple of dry amusement in her voice left him breathless.

"Gotcha."

"It's really nice of you to ask," she said.

He licked his lips. "Do you—"

"Max," she said hurriedly, interrupting him. "I can't. We can't."

He sighed. She was right, and he knew it. No matter what he wanted to think about what life might be like when his guardianship was finalized, she was Mia's caseworker and everything about what he felt for her was wildly inappropriate. She could lose her job.

Fuck, he could lose Mia if he weren't careful. But even if he didn't, even after Mia was completely his, Lizzie's job could still be at risk. It was her name on all of the paperwork; there were licenses and rules about this sort of thing. Just because the case wasn't active didn't mean she wasn't still responsible for it.

He scrubbed his hand over his face, realizing he needed to shave before he went to work. "We have to stop seeing each other."

"We're not seeing each other."

"We have to stop wanting to," he said dryly.

She let out a small noise that sounded suspiciously like a snort. "I know."

"I'm going to find another babysitter for Wednesday nights." It was what he had to do, to pull them back onto a purely professional level.

She let out a long, slow breath. "That's ... probably a good idea."

"All right. Have a good Thanksgiving, Lizzie." He had to end this now, before he tried to reach through the phone to pull her to him.

"You too, Max."

TWO WEEKS LATER, he called her again. "I'm not missing the irony here," he said before she could say anything. "I realize that inviting you to a party is literally the opposite of what we both said I should be doing, but I swear it's not like that."

"You're inviting me to a party in a professional capacity?" He could picture her blonde eyebrows rising, her eyes narrowing, the slight smile on those lips he couldn't quite get out of his head.

"I really am."

"I don't think I've ever been to a party that involved work for a case," she said.

"There's a time for everything," he told her. "Look, you need to verify that my childcare situation is taken care of, and that Mia is settling in and has a solid social life and support network here, right?"

"Yeeesss," she said slowly. "But I'm not sure where you're going with this."

"My friend Angelica is hosting her annual holiday decorating party. Literally everybody Mia loves is going to be there, her whole support system. You can come, see how they interact with her in a social setting, not a forced interview."

There was silence, and he crossed his fingers as he leaned back in his chair. He was in his office at Frankie's, a small room up the back stairs tucked into the eave of what most people assumed was just a decorative gable overlooking River Hill's town square. He didn't enjoy the time he spent locked up here seeing to paperwork, but he loved to sit and look out his window and watch people walk together through the square. He'd seen an entire Hallmark movie marathon's worth of romantic moments in the gazebo that anchored the green space of the town square.

"I suppose that makes sense," she said slowly.

"I promise, I won't even come near you."

She huffed out a small laugh. "I don't need a restraining order, Max."

I might. She still lived in his dreams every night, though he was getting better at putting her in the 'fantasy' category instead of the 'possibility' one. "Just making sure you can do your job without me bothering you, I swear. I don't want anything to mess up Mia's progress."

"All right. When is this party?"

"Friday night at The Oakwell Inn. We're all getting together to help decorate it for the holidays. It's a good time."

"That's that B&B in town, right? The one that opened a couple of years ago?"

"Yeah."

"Wait. Isn't that owned by—your friend is Angelica Travis? The *actress*?" Her voice rose slightly at the end of her question. It was easy to forget that Angelica was a bonafide celebrity, until someone who didn't know her figured out who she was, surprise coloring their realization that she was his close friend.

"I thought you knew. Hasn't Mia mentioned her?"

Lizzie laughed, the warm burble running through his veins like a shot of espresso. "The only one I hear about is your friend Naomi. I hear they're doing some kind of art project together."

"Yeah, Mia's gotten the ultimate stamp of approval. She's actually been invited to Naomi's studio, which is a minor miracle. There's like three people allowed in there, total."

"She's a very talented artist, Max."

"I know. Naomi told me. At length."

Another chuckle. "I'm glad she's found a mentor."

"You'll see what else she has when you come to the party," Max said smugly. He'd performed the ultimate childcare coup, in his opinion.

"I'll be there."

HE WAS SO busy watching Mia with Angelica's mom that he almost missed Lizzie's entrance. Maeve met her at the door and brought her to the parlor, where Noah was balancing Mia on his shoulder so that she could set the star on top of the tree. Elaine Travis was directing the entire affair with the patient air of a grandmother, even though she wasn't one yet. Not for lack of trying on Noah's part, Max suspected.

Without a grandchild of her own, Elaine had taken to Mia—and vice versa—like a house on fire, and now the Travis matriarch was firmly ensconced in his and Mia's lives. She and her husband had arrived to help out at The Oakwell at Thanksgiving, and would be staying for the next six months or so. They'd spent every winter in River Hill since Angelica had opened her B&B, helping run it while she was off filming her show, and now they were thinking about making the move permanent.

He hoped they did. His own parents were long gone, and since his grandparents were frail and living in Argentina, he hadn't thought he'd be able to provide Mia with this sort of grandmotherly affection. But Elaine mothered all of them indiscriminately, and he found himself enjoying it almost as much as Mia did. And best of all, Elaine had offered to take on Wednesday babysitting before he could even ask.

"Let me introduce you around," he said to Lizzie. "Then I'll back off."

She smiled at him, and he exerted firm control on his body to keep himself from leaning forward to take her into his arms. Still, he gave himself permission to take his fill of her with his eyes. Covertly, of course. She wore a slim black skirt over black tights and knee-high boots, topped by a cream sweater that looked impossibly soft. Her blonde hair was loose over her shoulders, and he'd seen a glimpse of sparkling earrings in the shape of snowflakes. She was like a walking holiday commercial, and he wanted to buy anything she was selling. He shook off the effect she had on him, and led her over to the tree.

"Obviously you already know Mia."

"Hi Lizzie!" His niece waved from her perch on Noah's shoulders. The winemaker was inevitably the tallest man in any room, and his large frame made him seem even bigger. He generally had to make a concerted effort not to loom, but today it made him the perfect ladder. Mia had moved on from the star to hanging delicate glass orbs near the top of the tree, one of which she shook playfully at Max.

"Be careful with that," he cautioned. "It's probably fancy."

"Isn't everything?" Noah rumbled.

"Lizzie Teague, this is Noah Bradstone, Angelica's fiancé. He owns the vineyard you drove through to get here."

"Nice to meet you," Lizzie murmured next to him.

"I'm Elaine Travis, Angelica's mom." Predictably, Elaine beat him to the punch. Angelica was an apple that hadn't fallen very far from the maternal tree. "You must be the social services caseworker."

"I am."

"It's great to meet you," Elaine enthused. "Thanks for all of your help with Mia. She's so wonderful."

"Elaine has taken on some babysitting duties," Max said quietly. Lizzie's eyes shot to his, and he saw that she understood.

"Come meet the rest of the gang," he said. "Then

Angelica will probably put you to work. I hope you like hanging garland."

She raised her hands, the light dusting of pale glitter on her nails sparkling in the lamp light. "My uncle owns an antique store. I'm practically a hanging-things-up expert."

"Exactly what I want to hear," said Angelica from behind him. "Max, go away. I'm taking over immediately."

He laughed and surrendered. "Angelica Travis, Lizzie Teague. She's better at introductions than I am, anyway."

He watched as Lizzie got swept up in Angelica's inevitable charm offensive, and grinned as she kept her cool while being shuffled quickly from group to group. Somehow, even with Angelica's oversized personality, Lizzie managed to fit right in. Naomi made room for her at the table where she and Jess were assembling some sort of complicated pinecone-based centerpiece, and Lizzie's laughter soon mingled with the rest of the group's.

He caught his breath, feeling a pinpoint of pain in his chest that swiftly grew to an ache. This—this was perfect. He'd brought her here in a professional capacity, trying to prove to her that he was doing fine, that he didn't need her anymore. That he had this whole parenting thing down. But watching her with his friends made his entire plan seem like a flimsy ploy. He wanted her here. With him. And Mia.

Even with the risk, he wanted her. And he wanted to do whatever it took to convince her it would all be okay.

Somehow.

It had to be.

8
___

Several days later, Lizzie took a small sip of some seriously delicious zinfandel, admiring its deep, jammy color as the glass came away from her lips, the liquid glinting in the lamp light. "This is really good."

All things considered, she didn't have many vices, but Uncle Horatio's deep love of everything vintage included vintage wines, and she'd learned to share his opinions. Living in wine country these past couple of years, she'd developed an appreciation for the varietals that were most common to the area, zinfandel chief among them.

"Thanks," Angelica said, refilling her own glass before standing up and making her way toward the kitchen. "It comes from a small vintner a few miles down the road," she called out over her shoulder as she crossed out of sight.

"I thought I heard Noah saying he grew zinfandel?" Lizzie said to the rest of the gathered women. She'd enjoyed the conversations at the holiday party, and learned a lot about this group of friends. She'd been surprised by the invitation to join Angelica's romance novel book club today, but happy to receive it.

Maeve gestured over her shoulder with her thumb. "Just up the hill behind the inn, in fact, but they're still in their infancy. You should ask Angelica about that." She smirked, and Jess tittered.

"What do you mean?" she asked.

"Let's just say those vines are the result of Angelica and Noah's very own meet-cute."

"Meet-cute?"

"You know," Jess explained, her tone indicating she couldn't believe Lizzie wasn't familiar with the term. "It's when a couple meets for the first time and the situation leads to an inevitable romance." She leaned forward in her seat and dropped her voice low. "Given her Hollywood connections, Angelica pretends to hate it when we say this, but her and Noah's story would make the perfect Netflix rom-com, right down to his goofy old dog, Molly."

"They were cursing each other out within minutes of meeting," Naomi said.

"Really?" Lizzie had a hard time reconciling that with the lovey-dovey couple she'd met a handful of days before. Noah was clearly smitten with his bombshell fiancée, and for her part, Angelica couldn't keep her admiration for Noah from shining through.

"Yup," the artist continued. "Believe it or not, Noah *hated* Angelica. Or rather, he wanted to. But the second he said her name to me, I knew he was a goner. That man had been looking for a woman like Angelica his whole damn life. He just didn't know it. It's your classic enemies-to-lovers trope brought to life."

"That's actually kind of sweet," Lizzie remarked, silently wondering if she'd ever have her own meet-cute. She didn't think taking one look at her client and immediately wanting to jump his bones qualified. "Are all of the books you read like that?"

"Not all of them. Take this book, for example." Maeve lifted the paperback they were discussing. Lizzie hadn't had time to read it, since her invitation to join them had been somewhat last minute, but apparently it was the story of a country music star who was on the run from a deranged fan, and the man assigned to be her bodyguard. According to Naomi, it was the sexiest book she'd read all year. "I don't typically read dark romance, but what I appreciated about this one was how the author flipped the script, so to speak. It's common to have a tortured hero, but in this case it's the *heroine* who is a recovering alcoholic with a series of one night stands in her past. That's actually how she first meets the hero. Suffice it to say, theirs is *not* a meet-cute."

"No, it doesn't sound like it," Lizzie said, thumbing through the pages of the copy Angelica had lent her. Honestly, she wasn't sure it sounded all that romantic, but if it had Maeve's seal of approval, how bad could it be? Still ... "Historically, I haven't really read a lot of romance. Maybe I should start with something a bit lighter."

Naomi chuckled and poured herself a glass of chardonnay. "Neither had I. If you'd have asked me what I thought of them before Angelica basically forced them on me, I'd have said they were trite at best, garbage at worst, and that they sell women an unrealistic view of what romance is. I mean, not every relationship has to end with a wedding and a baby." She crossed her arms over her chest in a defensive posture. Naomi might be outspoken about how solid her relationship with Iain Brennan was, but underneath that bravado, Lizzie could sense an aura of vulnerability, too.

Not that she couldn't understand why. Lizzie knew all too well how society expected women of a certain age—her age, to be exact—to be married already with two-point-five kids and a Subaru in the driveway. A white picket fence was just the icing on the cake.

"Which is why the books we read are more inclusive than you'd have found in the past," Jess added.

"That's the beauty of romance," Angelica said as she floated into the room carrying a tray of appetizers. "Happily-ever-after comes in many forms, and the only hard and fast rule for the genre is that there is one."

"That sounds pretty broad."

"You love Jane Austen, right?" Jess asked, popping a handful of almonds into her mouth.

Lizzie nodded. "Of course. Who doesn't?"

"Well there you go," Angelica said. "What's more romantic than Elizabeth and Darcy?"

Lizzie chuckled. "Honestly? Darcy is kind of a jerk to Elizabeth for most of the book."

Naomi nodded enthusiastically. "It's the enemies-to-lovers trope again."

"Hmm," Lizzie murmured, still somewhat skeptical. She'd only agreed to attend tonight because Angelica had assured her they spent more time eating and drinking than they did actually discussing the book they were supposed to have read.

Honestly, she'd been skeptical about the book club in general when Angelica had extended the invite. While she'd driven home from the holiday party with cheeks that ached from smiling so much, she'd been there as Mia's caseworker. Having firmly established that Max had created a stable and loving support system for his niece, she should have turned tonight's invitation down, but since moving to the Bay Area she'd formed zero legitimate friendships, and with the holidays looming, she was feeling more lonely than usual.

"Speaking of romance," Angelica said, settling down on the sofa next to Lizzie, her feet pulled up under her. "What's up with you and Max?"

Lizzie practically choked on her wine. Wiping a dribble of liquid from her chin, she turned wide eyes to her host. "What do you mean?"

Angelica waved a hand airily in front of her face. "Please. I saw you eyeing that mistletoe all night."

Across the circle, Naomi smiled like the cat who'd caught the canary. "God, I love Christmas."

"You're Jewish," Jess drawled.

Naomi simply shrugged her shoulders. "Give me a holiday that encourages making out with a sexy Irishman in dark corners, and I'm all for it."

"Eww," Maeve laughed.

"Oh, please," Naomi countered. "I saw Ben pulling you into the pantry, and I know you weren't looking for flour."

Maeve turned scarlet, but didn't deny the accusation.

"But back to Lizzie and Max," Angelica said pointedly. "Spill the beans, woman."

"There's really nothing to tell," Lizzie demurred.

"Been there, done that." Maeve fluttered her fingers as the rest of the women laughed. "How long did I insist that Ben and I were simply friends?"

Jess chuckled. "Months. Everyone saw it but you two."

Maeve nodded. "We wasted *a lot* of time fighting our attraction. I mean, we built a lovely friendship first, which I think is important, but—"

"But Max and I aren't even friends," Lizzie countered, attempting to cut the conversation off at the pass before it truly got away from her. "He's my client."

"And do you look at all your clients like that?" Angelica raised her eyebrow skeptically.

Lizzie schooled her features, pasting as innocent a look as she could muster on her face. "Like what?"

"Like you want to lick him!" Maeve and Naomi blurted in unison before erupting into peals of laughter.

Unbidden, Lizzie's memory flashed back to the first time she'd had that exact same thought. How many times since then had it echoed through her brain? The first time, she'd had the exquisite carbonara sauce as a scapegoat—not wanting to let good food go to waste, and all that. But now, whenever she saw Max, the first thing that inevitably sprang to mind was, *I want to climb this man like a tree and lick him from head to toe.*

Startling, since she'd never before thought anything even remotely similar about any man she'd ever known. Which probably explained why at thirty-four, she was perpetually single.

One thing she *didn't* dispute about the romance

novels these women loved to read so much was that passion was an essential part of any healthy relationship. And she hadn't felt even a fraction of the passion she felt for Max for anyone. Ever. And they'd never even kissed!

Not that they were ever going to.

Still, she could imagine how hot it would be.

Heck, *hot* didn't begin to describe what it would be like to be with Max. It would be explosive. Incendiary. Cataclysmic.

Just thinking about it had her growing hot under the collar—and elsewhere.

"See, that's what I'm talking about." Angelica twirled her index finger in front of Lizzie's heated face. "You've got it bad, girl."

Her shoulders slumped in on themselves. "Fine. You're right; I do. But we can't do anything about it. The rules are pretty clear. I could lose my license."

Jess swung her legs down from her chair to the floor and leaned forward, her fingers linked together between her legs. "What? Why?"

"Yeah, why?" Maeve echoed.

Lizzie blew out a long breath. "There's a whole lot of legalese I won't get into, but essentially it all boils down to it being a violation of professional ethics to engage in a sexual relationship with a client."

Naomi's brows dipped into a deep vee. "But *Mia's* your client; not Max."

"Technically, they're *both* my clients."

"Well that sucks," Jess mused, flopping back against the cushions.

"Yeah ..." Lizzie agreed with a sigh as she set her glass off to the side. "Even being here with you guys is walking a fine line. I should probably go." She pushed to her feet, and reached down to gather up her purse.

Before she'd had a chance to hoist it up onto her shoulder, the others were out of their seats, surrounding her with exclamations of disbelief and support.

"What? No! Don't go."

"That's ridiculous!"

"You're fucking kidding me."

"Please stay."

One by one, she took in these funny, warm, amazingly supportive woman, her chest tightening with the knowledge that she was going to miss them. Between the holiday party and tonight's book club, realistically, she'd only known them for a handful of hours, but even in that short amount of time she'd had the sort of affirming, fulfilling conversations every woman wanted out of her friends.

Assuming she had female friends in the first place.

Unfortunately for Lizzie, outside of Maggie, friendships were in relatively short supply these days. Sure, she'd kept in touch with a few women she'd gone to college with via Facebook and Instagram, but it had been ages since she'd sat down with another woman and just ... *relaxed*. Had a conversation that wasn't about work or her boss. Frankly, it was surprising to Lizzie that this group dynamic seemed to work so well. Angelica, Naomi, Jess, and Maeve were all very different, and yet they'd formed a tight-knit circle—one they'd been willing to expand to include her.

It both warmed her heart, and slightly broke it at the same time.

She smiled wanly. "I appreciate this; really, I do. But it's inappropriate for me to form any sort of relationship with the people in Mia and Max's life. If we'd met under different circumstances, maybe things would be different ... maybe Max and I could actually be together, and we could all be friends—"

Angelica held up her hand. "Look. I won't begin to say that I know what you're dealing with, but I think I speak for all of us when I say we *do* know what it's like to be conflicted about a man, and how he could ever fit into our lives. If nothing else, maybe just talking about it will help you feel better. Not to psychoanalyze you or anything, but it's kind of obvious you've been keeping your feelings bottled up. The anxiety practically radiates off of you."

And here Lizzie thought she'd been doing an admirable job of keeping her emotions under wraps. "Is it really that obvious?"

Three heads bobbed up and down as Naomi moved around the coffee table and toward Lizzie, picking up her discarded glass along the way and passing it back to her. "It should go without saying, but book club is sacred. Nothing you say outside of this circle will be repeated."

Jess cleared her throat. "I mean, I tell Sean everything."

Maeve chuckled nervously. "Um, Ben demands a full run down when I get home."

Lizzie turned to Angelica, who was smirking. "Noah's the worst gossip of them all."

Naomi wrapped her arm around Lizzie's shoulder and led her back to her seat. "We'll swear them to secrecy, though." She said it like she had every expectation the promise would be kept by everyone, even those who weren't here, and somehow Lizzie believed her.

Lizzie knew she should head to the door, but for the first time in years, she felt a part of something bigger than she was. She felt ... like she belonged. How could she resist this kind of friendship, when it was being extended to her in spite of everything? It was reasonable to expect her not to date her clients; but surely she was allowed to have a *friend* or two, once in a while. So even though every part of her brain was screaming at her to get the hell out of dodge, she let herself be swept up in the warmth and acceptance these women had extended to her without expecting anything in return.

With a weary sigh, she fell back into her seat and scanned the circle, deciding that just for tonight she'd put her career aside and just be a woman, falling for a man, who wanted advice from her girlfriends. Tomorrow she'd do the right thing for her career. Right now, though, she was doing the right thing for her soul. "I like him so much, you know? Why does he have to be so amazing?"

9

"Ou invited Lizzie to the New Year's Eve party?" Max stared at Angelica, who smirked at him. "Are you trying to get me in trouble?"

She waved her hand dismissively. "Relax. I invited her as my friend, not your ... whatever."

"But—"

"Or are you saying she's not allowed to have friends?" She arched an eyebrow at him and he scowled back at her.

"You're meddling, Angelica Travis," he accused.

"Pretty rich, coming from you," she shot back.

"What are you talking about?"

"Max, you've meddled in all of our lives." She held up a perfectly manicured finger. "With good results, I'll grant you, but you're practically a yenta."

"What's a yenta?"

She grinned at him. "You ever seen 'Fiddler on the Roof'?" She sang a few lines. Badly. "Matchmaker, matchmaker, make me a match!"

"Stop. Please." Angelica might have been a movie star once, but musicals were definitely *not* her forte.

She stuck out her tongue at him. "My point stands. You're the king of meddlers, Max Vergaras, and you're just mad that somebody's doing it to you for once."

"I'm not mad," he protested. "Maybe a little annoyed. Mostly worried. She could lose her license, Angelica."

"Then keep your hands off her, Max," his friend said sweetly.

Two hours later, he was resenting Angelica furiously for that little dig. Because keeping his hands off Lizzie was the hardest thing he'd ever done. She'd arrived a little late, the last member of their merry band to gather.

Angelica's New Year's party was starting to become infamous. Last year, Sean and Jess had shown up to it and announced that they were married after eloping in Costa Rica. This year, they'd announced they were expecting a baby. From the looks on several faces, it wasn't exactly a surprise. Angelica had simply rolled her eyes and reminded Jess that her bridesmaid dress had an empire waist already, and the other women had all laughed.

Lizzie had laughed too, but it had seemed a bit ... off. Max hadn't realized he knew her well enough to know when she was faking it—*and let's head that thought off at the pass*, he reminded himself. But she wasn't her usual, cheerful self, and he thought he might not be the only one who noticed.

Angelica and Maeve were both shooting her frequent worried glances. In Angelica's case, they were accompanied by an occasional laser-eyed glare in his direction, which he met with a scowl of his own. *He* hadn't done anything. And her hands-off ultimatum meant that he didn't dare approach Lizzie to try to find out what was wrong either, since he wasn't entirely sure he could stop himself from just gathering her up into his arms and kissing her worries away.

Forcing himself not to hover, he got busy pulling another tray of canapes out of The Oakwell's oversized pantry fridge—Angelica had added space for catering storage the year after she'd opened the place, and now events at the inn were increasingly popular. She was even planning to have her own wedding here. In fact, some of the appetizers he'd put together for the party tonight were ones he was proposing for her wedding menu; he wasn't above killing two birds with one culinary stone.

"Want some help?" It was Ben, leaning against the door of the pantry.

"Sure. But don't pretend you're not just here for the figs with goat cheese."

"You know me too well," his best friend said.

Max handed him the platter, and he snagged a fig from the edge and popped it into his mouth. "Hey," Ben said around the mouthful of cheesy goodness. "Are you okay?"

"Of course I am." Max shut the door of the refrigerator with more force than he intended, and it promptly bounced back open. "Dammit."

"Max."

"What?" he snapped as he closed the fridge again, more carefully this time. "I'm fine. Can't imagine what you're asking about."

It was a futile endeavor to try to fool Ben. They'd been friends since elementary school, and Max had spent more time with Ben's family than he had with his own. After his and Isabel's parents had died, Ben's mom had taken them even further under her wing. He still exchanged holiday cards with her every year. Ten years ago she'd started including a chatty family newsletter detailing all the various ways her children were exceptional human beings. Last year, when Ben had lost his job and had moved into the apartment over Max's garage while he got his life back on track, Max had cheekily signed his own card 'Love, Max and Ben.' This year, Ben's mom's newsletter had been mostly full of news about Maeve, and Max had laughed out loud when he read it. Mrs. Worthington might love Ben's girlfriend even more than she loved her own son.

"Do you remember when you had that talk with me?" Ben asked.

"Can you be more specific?" He'd had a lot of talks with Ben, starting with serious debate over the possession of an aging soccer ball, through discussion of college courses and the various girls that might be met therein, all the way up through—

"The one where you warned me to get my shit together about Maeve."

"Ah, yeah. That one."

"Yeah. That one." Ben leaned toward him, the platter of figs between them. "Listen. Maeve says that Lizzie has been hanging out with the girls a lot. None of them are blind, you know. They all know which way the wind is blowing, so to speak."

"There's no wind," Max grumbled. "Weather here all perfectly sunny and clear."

"You can't bullshit a bullshitter, Max." Ben had been a highly successful corporate attorney before he moved to River Hill, making a name for himself in some very high-powered courtroom cases. Now, he had his own practice, his clients primarily the small businesses that made up River Hill's town square and commercial district—Max included. But he still had all the instincts that had brought him to the top of the heap. "You and Lizzie have something going on, and it's getting messy."

"I can't," Max said. "She can't. *We* can't. I could lose Mia. She could lose her job. You're right, it's messy."

"Then, if you will pardon the repetition, get your shit together." Ben frowned. "You're either in or you're out, and it isn't fair to her to keep this longing gaze from across the room thing going."

"I'm not—"

"Trust me, you are."

"I'm trying not to."

Ben balanced the platter of figs on one hand and freed the other one to poke him in the chest. "Try harder. That girl is a ball of stress, and if any of it is your fault, you're going to hate yourself as much as everyone else will hate you." He was speaking from experience, Max knew.

"I'll figure something out," he said. "Take those figs to the dining room before you eat them all."

Ben defiantly popped another tasty morsel into his mouth, eyeballing Max until he shoved the other man out the door with a reluctant laugh.

They rejoined the crowd, finding Angelica reigning supreme with wedding details while the TV on the wall showed a view of crowds in various cities waiting for the final midnight countdown, complete with musical performances in freezing outdoor arenas and shivering hosts wrapped in fuzzy coats pretending to be happy about it. Thank goodness they were in California. And indoors.

Max let his gaze roam the room, watching his friends with their partners. How had he managed to be the only single one? It was an increasingly unpleasant sensation, and it wasn't helped by the fact that the person he most wanted to remedy the situation with sat on the couch with the fakest smile he'd ever seen plastered across her beautiful face.

Get your shit together, Max. If she was going to be friends with his friends, he had to be able to be in the same room with her without wanting to strip her naked and claim her as his.

No time like the present to practice. He sat down next to her, careful to keep a little distance between their bodies. Every time he touched her he lost his mind, so the first step was not to touch her no matter how much his entire body screamed out for it.

"Happy New Year," he said.

"Thanks." She gave him a smile that was a little less fake than the one she'd been wearing for the last hour or so, but her eyes were still ringed with circles the smoky eye makeup she'd applied couldn't hide. "You too."

"Is ... is everything okay?" he blurted. "You seem—"

She shook her head, short and fast. "I'm fine."

She was definitely *not* fine. He frowned. "Lizzie, I know I'm not the person you want to talk about stuff with, but—"

She interrupted him with a laugh that bordered on hysterical. "Max, I'd absolutely love to spend all my time talking to you, but I can't. In fact, you're the *one* person I'd love to talk to about anything and everything." She winced. "Sorry. I didn't mean to say all that."

"I feel the same way," he said quietly. He missed the flirty texts and memes, and the quiet, late night conversations across his dining room table. "I like being friends with you, Lizzie, not just... you know. The other stuff."

"The stuff we're not talking about." She met his gaze, and there was humor lurking under the anxiety in her eyes.

"Yeah. That stuff."

She sighed. "Life just sometimes feels overwhelmingly unfair, you know?"

"Tell me about it," he said feelingly.

Her lips quirked. "At least you have a job you love."

He frowned. "Is work stuff—"

He was interrupted by a shriek from Jess. "It's starting!"

They both looked at the TV, which was showing the giant crystal ball in Times Square lit up at the top of its tower. The crowd in New York was shouting, "TEN! NINE! EIGHT!" as they counted down to midnight, and his friends were joining in. Noah had his arms around Angelica's waist, Maeve was in Ben's lap, Jess and Sean were wrapped up in each other, and

Naomi and Iain were jammed together on one of the upholstered armchairs. Everyone was smiling, and laughing, and counting aloud, and Max turned to look at Lizzie next to him on the couch.

Something in her face made him close the distance between them, something scared and hopeful and so, so perfect. He reached for her when the countdown got to five, and she leaned in toward him. *Bad idea, bad idea, bad idea* his mind was screaming as he slid his hands under all that silky hair, cupping her cheek and drawing her fully to him as the tinny voices on the TV merged with those of his friends to shout "...three! ... two! ...one!"

Her eyes were locked on his, and he watched them drift shut as his lips met hers. And then he stopped thinking at all. He'd been dreaming about the way she might taste for months. His imagination hadn't been up to the challenge. She was sweet vanilla, and starlit meadows, and the best French pastry he'd ever tasted, all rolled up with hints of savory spice and fresh air. Her lips softened against his briefly, then firmed as his tongue slid gently along their crease. She opened for him, and he was pretty sure the fireworks over the town square had taken up permanent residence in his body. And then her tongue slid against his, bold and strong, and he groaned and let his hand fall to her waist, gathering her against him.

Somehow, somewhere, people were talking, and someone was calling his name. "Max. Max!"

He pulled reluctantly away from Lizzie, watching her eyes open, the blue nearly swallowed by the black of her dilated pupils. "What?" he mumbled.

Lizzie blinked, and then he watched her draw away from him, her expression shifting rapidly from dazed arousal to familiar worry.

There was a hand on his arm. It was Angelica, her eyes dancing with both amusement and worry that matched Lizzie's. "Max. You promised."

He licked his lips and tried to force his voice to work. Lizzie's eyes followed the quick movement, and he felt his fingers tighten over her waist before she tugged herself free of his grasp. "It's New Year's. Everyone kisses at midnight."

"Not like that," Angelica said dryly.

He gave her a pointed look, then glanced around the room. Iain's hand was firmly ensconced on Naomi's ass, and Maeve and Ben were *still* kissing.

Angelica blew out a breath. "You can't—"

"It's okay," Lizzie said. She stood up, and Max reached for her without thinking. She evaded his hands and stepped back. "It was just a New Year's kiss." She darted a swift glance at him, and he knew they were both lying. "I need to go, though. Work stuff waits for no one." The smile she offered Angelica was wavering, and she didn't smile at Max at all. "I'll-I'll talk to you soon, okay?"

"Lizzie—" He stood, but she was already halfway to the door.

"I appreciate your technique, but your timing *sucks*," Angelica hissed at him. She hip-checked him, and he fell back onto the couch as she followed Lizzie out.

He was *fucked*. And not in the good way.

10

"*Coming up in the next hour, we've got our resident beauty expert Jessica Casillas-Moore in the studio to talk about all the tiny ways stress can manifest itself on your face, plus Professor Miranda Whitcomb-Talbot will be here to discuss her latest book, Your Boss is Sabotaging You. But first—*"

Lizzie stabbed the power button on her car radio to turn the damn thing off. She normally enjoyed Jess's beauty segments—even more so now that she knew her *outer* beauty was matched only by her *inner* beauty—but she didn't need to listen to her new friend outline all the ways that stress could impact one's looks. The woman staring back at her in the bathroom mirror this morning was proof enough. Between the dark smudges under her eyes from lack of sleep, and the patchy, broken skin on her hands and elbows, it was quite obvious that stress was to blame for her haggard appearance.

Try as Lizzie might, she hadn't been able to erase the memory of Max's kiss from her brain. In fact, she'd stayed up several nights in a row obsessing over it—how it impacted her career, what it meant for her future ... what it might mean for *their* future. She looked like she hadn't slept in days because she hadn't.

And when she wasn't asking herself those Very Important Questions, she let herself imagine what would have happened if Angelica hadn't interrupted them. Would he have laid her down on the couch and spread his big, hard body out over hers as he took the kiss deeper? Would he have trailed kisses past her jaw and down her neck until he reached the rise of her breast propped up by the sexiest bra she owned—the one she never wore because it was akin to a torture device? Would he have slid his hand up her calf and under her skirt, pulling her thigh up around his waist as he rolled his hips against her?

No. She shook her head and refocused her eyes on the road as her core pulsed with aching need. Which reminded her—she needed to stop and get more batteries on her drive home, because lord knew that was all she could ever have of Max. Just her memories, her vibrator, and a very active imagination to see her through the cold winter nights stretching out ahead of her.

The party had been her private goodbye to the Vergaras family. To the whole River Hill gang, in fact.

Because as it turned out, Lizzie didn't need to listen to a radio segment asking whether or not your boss was trying to sabotage you. She was living proof of that, too.

Maggie had been warning Lizzie for months that Kate had it in for her, but she'd mostly ignored her colleague, hoping that it would all pass. Lately, though, it had been getting harder and harder to pretend that Maggie wasn't right. And now, Lizzie had received a so-called "promotion" she'd neither asked for, nor wanted.

Twenty minutes before closing down the office for the holiday, Kate had pulled Lizzie aside and informed her that she'd be taking on a new role within the agency. A role, Lizzie seethed as she lay on her horn as an oversized pickup truck cut her off, that took everything she enjoyed about her job and replaced it with tedious paperwork better suited to an administrator. Essentially, everything Kate hated about her own job had been unceremoniously dumped on Lizzie—including a one-hundred-mile commute *each way* to and from Sacramento multiple times a week.

She'd been tempted to quit right there on the spot, but her conscience had forced her to bite her tongue and calmly walk out the door before she said something she'd regret. She'd had a party to go home and get dressed for.

Only now, she was rethinking her supposedly sensible decision to not tell Kate to take her promotion and shove it where the sun didn't shine.

She'd been on the road for nearly three hours and had only made it as far as Davis, and if the line of cars stretching out in front of her as far as the eye could see was any indication, she was going to be stuck here a lot longer.

With a resigned sigh, she turned the radio back on.

Some are calling it a post-Christmas miracle, but for the thousands of commuters stranded on the freeway, it's more like a nightmare. We're going live to Sacramento where a major winter snowstorm has brought the city to a standstill. Mike, what's it like where you are?

A snow storm? In Sacramento? Granted, she wasn't originally from the area, but she'd lived in Northern California long enough to know that snow below the foothills wasn't a regular occurrence. In fact, the bigger problem had always been a *lack* of snow in these parts. Low snowpack in the Sierras meant no spring melt, which inevitably led to drought conditions in the summer ... which, more and more frequently, meant wildfires in late summer and early fall. Unfortunately, she'd seen first-hand the emotional toll the last fire storm had wrought when she'd been assigned to a group of siblings who'd lost their parents and their home at the same time. It had been one of the hardest cases Lizzie had ever worked, but by the time their aunt and uncle had formally adopted the three kids, all were on their way to healing—as much as one ever could from that sort of tragedy.

At the memory of that case, Lizzie felt a sharp pinch from somewhere behind her breastbone. Unconsciously, she rubbed the heel of her palm back and forth over the vicinity of her heart, pushing down hard when another sharp pain stole her breath. In an effort to try and calm her emotions, she zeroed in on the voices coming out of her speakers. She had enough experience with anxiety to know she wasn't having a heart attack, but she also knew that if she didn't get hold of her emotions, she could spiral into a full-blown panic attack—and that was the last thing she needed right now.

Emergency responders are dealing with a twelve-car pile up on Highway 80 at Auburn, as well as a four-car accident just outside of Roseville. Caltrans is asking motorists to stay home if at all possible as conditions are expected to deteriorate even further as the freak storm heads south.

The report continued as Lizzie scanned the horizon. Traffic was complete chaos with motorists honking and yelling at one another as they tried to move into the far right lane to exit the freeway. Squaring her shoulders, she girded her proverbial loins and flicked on her blinker, ready to enter the fray herself when her phone rang through her car's Bluetooth speakers. Glancing over her shoulder, she ignored the ringing and nosed her way into the next lane, lifting her hand in silent *thanks* to the driver now behind her. When she'd made her way across two more lanes, the ringing started anew.

"For fuck's sake," she muttered, the stress from the long drive and current traffic situation causing her to let loose an uncharacteristic expletive. It was one of Max's favorite sayings, a fact she tried to ignore as it came out of her own mouth. She pressed the button on her steering wheel to send the call through.

"Hello?" she asked, spying a break in traffic wide enough that she could slip between two semis and exit the freeway.

"Elizabeth," a shrill voice sounded through the speakers.

"I'm a little busy, Kate."

"Well, I can't imagine with what since I know you missed the meeting with David and Thomas. I just got off the phone with them and—"

"Kate, I'm kind of dealing with a mess here."

"Well, now I'm dealing with *your* mess, so—"

Lizzie didn't know if it was the sleepless nights, the stress of this new job, her pining over Max, or all of the above, but as she swung into the next lane and slammed her foot down on the gas pedal, sending her car skyrocketing down the exit ramp, Kate's voice and the complaints that came with it receded until the only thing Lizzie heard was the whirring of the blood in her veins and a dull pounding in her skull. She flipped a left at the light, then another left onto the onramp going in the opposite direction, and pointed her car toward home with a vicious twist of her wrist on the wheel.

"Listen, Kate. I should have said this before, and I'm sorry I didn't, but I don't want this job." She took a deep breath and plunged on, letting the words pour out of her mouth in steady progression toward an end result her brain was only just now catching up to. "I'm not an administrator; I'm a caseworker. My clients are what make getting up every morning and coming into work worth it. Without them, I'm just a paper pusher, and while that might be good enough for you, it's not good enough for me. It's not what I signed up for, and it's something I'm not willing to do."

As she spoke, Kate kept trying to interject with cries of "Wait!" and "Elizabeth!" and "You cannot do this!" but Lizzie wouldn't let her get a word in edgewise. She knew if she let her boss speak, the other woman would try to talk her out of what she was about to do, and since she hadn't thought this through very well—or at all, she conceded—there was a strong likelihood she'd capitulate to Kate's demands. So she kept going, hardly believing what she was saying herself as she settled into a steady speed in the opposite direction. "I know this isn't very professional, and I'm guessing this means you won't be giving me a reference—"

Kate snorted loudly, and Lizzie could practically picture her blue shadowed eye rolling up into the back of her head. "I should think not! You're lucky I haven't fired you for your insubordination before now, what with—"

What? Her insubordination? What insubordination? Until right this very second Lizzie had been a model employee.

Her fingers tightened on the steering wheel until her knuckles turned white. Unless Kate knew about how she'd kissed Max. Was that why she'd taken all of Lizzie's cases away from her? Had someone reported her for an ethics violation? Just as quickly, she shook her head. No, this was all Kate.

"I knew you couldn't handle my job," her boss—soon-to-be *former* boss—continued as Lizzie's attention was yanked back to the conversation. "I told Malcom that you're an ungrateful upstart who thinks you know better than anyone else."

"I'm *what*?" Lizzie squawked, her voice rising with shock. She'd always known she wasn't Kate's *favorite* employee, but never in a million years would she have thought Kate would describe her that way. She'd spent years helping to build their office's reputation as one of the best in the county, and until Max and Mia came along, she'd never set a foot wrong.

"You heard me," Kate fired back. "I tried protecting

you, Elizabeth, because that's what was best for the agency, but I should have known the second I gave you real responsibility you'd—"

Lizzie had had enough.

Enough of the constant put-downs.

Enough of the late nights with no appreciation.

Enough of the petty, back-handed compliments.

Enough of her job.

Enough of putting everyone and everything ahead of her own wants and desires.

Enough of denying herself the only man she'd ever wanted.

Enough pretending that Max and Mia weren't the family she'd secretly wished for at every major holiday.

Enough. Enough. Enough.

A sense of renewed purpose settled over her as she made a decision. A huge, scary, life-altering decision. She'd already made it, really, but now she knew, with every particle of her being, that it was the *right* choice. All around her, everything was chaos—cars swerving on the increasingly slippery road surface, her wipers furiously batting away big, fat wet flakes of snow—but in her head, everything had gone quiet. Calm.

"I'm sorry, Kate, but this conversation is over. Consider this my resignation, effective immediately. Now, if you'll excuse me, please go fuck yourself." Lizzie pressed the button on her steering wheel, ending the call. The second the line went quiet, all the precious calm that had previously flooded her system went flying out the window.

"Oh my god. What have I done?" Her pulse spiked and her breath came in staccato bursts as her anxiety mounted. "I have a mortgage. I can't go without a paycheck."

She was jobless, and she'd just told her best possible reference to go fuck herself. Never in the history of ever had she'd said those words to anyone— not even in the quiet of her mind when she was having one of those Ally McBeal dancing baby moments.

Suddenly, and without warning, a crazed laugh bubbled up from her chest and burst from between her lips. "I'm so screwed," she whispered aloud as the realization of what she'd just done settled over her. She drummed her fingers on the steering wheel in time with the beat in her head. *I'm so screwed, I'm so screwed, I'm so screwed.*

A handful of hours later, she'd somehow made her way to River Hill, and was inching her way down Max's street, the deepening snow slowing her progress. She had no recollection of how she'd decided to come here instead of heading home, but it was too late now. She couldn't get to her place even if she wanted to: the man on the radio had just announced they'd closed the road leading to her subdivision when a tree had fallen, bringing down the power lines with it. Anyone who wasn't already tucked up safe and sound inside their home was being directed to the nearby high school until the storm passed.

Eventually, she pulled into his long driveway, her hands clenching the steering wheel in a vice-like grip. Her heart was attempting to beat its way outside her chest, and her brain was yelling at her that being here was a mistake. But even as her mind tried to talk her out of it, she pulled her car to a stop next to his Land Rover and opened her door. Putting one foot in front of the other, she picked her way down his icy front walk and raised her hand to ring the doorbell. Thank god he was home. She hadn't even considered that he might be stuck at the restaurant. It was technically still dinnertime.

She tapped her freezing foot against the flagstones, counting down the seconds until he opened the door. She had no idea what she was going to say when he did. What she was going to *do*. All she knew was that she had to see him. Had to tell him what she'd done. So much of their relationship had been about *her* guiding *him* when he'd felt cut adrift. Now she needed him to return the favor.

The lock flipped on the other side of the heavy wooden door, and Lizzie's heart rocketed straight from the pit of her belly up into her throat, practically cutting off her air. Two seconds later, the door swung open, and Max stood there, his hair askew and a confused expression on his face.

"Lizzie?"

"Max," she breathed out, at a loss for any further words.

"Are you okay?" Without waiting for her response, he stepped out of the way and hurried her inside.

She hadn't realized how cold she was until a blast of heat from his fireplace enveloped her in its warmth. Her teeth chattering, she shook her head no, but her lips formed the word *yes*.

Max set his palms on her biceps and tipped his head forward to stare in her eyes. "What's wrong, sweetheart?"

She licked her lips as her gaze bounced over his handsome face. The eyes she could get lost in. The cleft of his chin that she dreamed about kissing. The tiny scar just above his right eyebrow she'd learned he got in college when he and Ben had botched a fraternity dare and wound up in the emergency room instead. The lips she now knew the taste of.

"I quit my job, Max."

He dropped his hands from her arms. "You did? When?"

"Just now," she answered, that same calmness she'd felt earlier returning.

"That's ... wow." He blew out a breath and ran his hand through his hair, a gesture she was coming to think of as so uniquely *him*. "Are you okay?"

Lizzie nodded, and felt a smile tilting her lips up and to the side. She wasn't stupid. Her life was about to become very difficult, but standing here right now, in front of the man she was crazy about, she knew somehow she'd be okay. For the first time since she'd hung up on Kate, she was positive something better was around the corner. She didn't know what it was, or how she'd find it, but if she was lucky, she'd have Max by her side the entire time.

"What does this mean?" His hands flexed at his sides ... as if he was fighting the instinct to touch her again. She lifted her face to his. "It means a lot of things that I'll have to think about eventually, but right now, it means you can kiss me."

"Thank fuck," he said, tugging her forward and planting his mouth on her, his tongue slipping between her lips to slide against her own.

Thank fuck, indeed, she thought as she wound her arms around his neck and finally climbed him like a tree.

11

They stumbled toward the living room, wrapped around each other, and Max lost all sense of who, when, and where he was. Lizzie's tongue matched his, stroking him to heights he'd never imagined. That New Year's kiss was *nothing* compared to this. He bumped into the back of the couch and her full weight came against him, her legs wrapping around him as he lifted her into his arms.

It wasn't until her cold hands snuck under his shirt that he had enough of a shock to his system to realize what was happening. He pulled away reluctantly. "Wait."

Her lips traveled to his neck, biting gently at the spot where his throat met his shoulder

He groaned. "Lizzie. Wait a minute."

"Hmm?" She licked him. Straight up his neck, like he was a popsicle.

He grabbed her wandering hands. "Stop for a second."

She finally pulled her head back. "You have to be kidding," she breathed, dropping her legs down to stand on her own two feet.

"No, I'm serious." He closed his eyes briefly as she shifted against him.

"What—" her eyes widened, and if he hadn't been so horny and confused he would have laughed at the way she looked wildly around in comic dismay. "Oh, my god. Mia. Where is she? I shouldn't … we shouldn't—"

"Relax," he said quickly. "She's spending the night at Maeve's. I was supposed to be working late tonight since Wendy had her nephew's bar mitzvah. But I closed early once the weather started getting bad." The perks of being the owner. Guests had stopped showing up once the weather people had started talking about the predicted movement of this crazy storm. With no one to serve, he'd sent his staff home before packing up a few essentials and getting out of there himself. He'd only just gotten home a few minutes before Lizzie had shown up at his door, and the short drive from the center of town had been nightmarish already. He couldn't imagine what hers had been like.

Normally, he would have been celebrating the fact that she'd decided to ride the storm out with him, but something wasn't quite right. "Lizzie. What's happening? We need to talk about this."

"Noooo," she said slowly. "We need to get naked."

An image of her body bared to him flashed behind his eyes and he felt himself harden. "God. Lizzie. Wait."

She frowned at him. "Why?"

"Did you quit your job because of me?" He gestured between them. "Because of this? I can't—I can't be the reason you quit, Lizzie." He felt his teeth clench. "That's not fair to either of us."

She stepped fully away from him then, and he felt the loss of her body against his as keenly as if someone had just cut off his own arm. "It's not like that," she said. "Not really."

He frowned. "What do you mean?" Her answer wasn't the confident 'No, of course not, Max' he'd expected.

She sighed and walked around the couch to sit down on it, unwinding her scarf the rest of the way and then shrugging out of her jacket. She tossed both on the arm of the couch as he sat down next to her, not bothering to keep space between them this time. Their thighs lined up, touching along the full length of their legs, and she leaned into him. He wrapped an arm around her and tugged her back to settle comfortably into the couch, letting the warmth from the fireplace heat them both through. Not that he needed much heating after that kiss. He was practically sweating already.

Slowly, she explained her job situation. How her boss had been undermining her from the start, impatient and demanding and ineffective all at the same time. How budget cuts had meant it had gotten harder and harder to help the kids she'd started her career for. And then, the final straw: her boss had taken away all of her cases—including Mia's—in some bid to make her an administrative minion.

"She sounds pretty awful," Max said, wrapping a curl of her hair around his finger, marveling at the softness of it. "But—"

"It's not just her," Lizzie interrupted. "It's all of it."

He couldn't resist. He leaned in and smelled her hair. "All of what?" She smelled like tropical fruit, and he pictured the two of them sipping fresh squeezed juice on a beach somewhere. Maybe it was the increasingly colder temperatures that winter brought, but Lizzie in a bikini was one of his favorite fantasies these days. And now it was starting to sound like he might actually get to see it someday.

Assuming this all actually went somewhere, and she wasn't just here to … what, bang out her frustrations? Get him out of her system? He chewed his lip. He didn't think that was where they'd been heading all this time, but he also hadn't expected her to up and quit her job unexpectedly.

"It's..." she frowned. "I really wasn't planning on thinking about all of this today, you know."

"Sorry." He wasn't really sorry, and it probably showed in his voice, because she poked him in the ribs. "Ow."

"There's a lot to it, okay? Yes, there was a breaking point in that I was three hours into a drive that I shouldn't have even been making. I missed the meeting I was supposed to be driving to in the first place, and then there's Kate taking all of my cases away. I knew going in that a big part of this work was documentation. But it seems like there's been more and more, and it's increasingly difficult to get to a point where you're able to take any action to help anybody. The truth is, I'm not sure this is what I want to do anymore." She bit her lip. "I hadn't realized it until now, is all."

"What *do* you want to do?"

"In the future? I don't know. Right now?" She pulled away from him, and he had one brief, heart-stopping moment to regret the choices he'd made since he'd stopped kissing her before his brain short circuited and started a hasty reboot process.

Because she'd just pulled off her shirt.

"I. Uh." His tongue felt like it was sticking to the roof of his mouth. He tried to yank it free and realized he was panting. Actually panting, like a dog. "Lizzie."

She grinned at him, a slow curve of her lips leading up to sparkling blue eyes that held none of the worry and stress she'd been radiating every time he'd seen her lately. She was nothing short of spectacular. "I think right now, we should get naked and see what happens."

"But—"

She put a hand on his chest and he froze. "Listen. I've been reading quite a few romance novels lately."

He blinked. It was such a nonsequitur that he found himself able to tear his gaze away from the view of her breasts cupped in perfect cream lace and back up to her face. "What?"

"I was pretty dubious about them, but it turns out that what they're really about is women standing up for themselves and taking what they want. And right now, Max, I want you."

"Feeling's mutual," he managed to croak.

"Then you're wearing too many clothes."

The next few seconds were a blur.

Somehow, they made it to the bedroom, shedding clothes in a trail he was going to have to remember to pick up before Mia got home. He tumbled her onto his bed, pausing for a moment to admire the sight of Lizzie sprawled against his sheets, eyes dark with desire as they looked him up and down. When her gaze took in his cock, he felt it harden even further and he groaned out loud. "You can't look at it like that."

She licked her lips and his knees buckled. He fell

forward onto the bed, bracing himself above her with his arms locked. She wrapped her legs around his waist and he gave up all pretense of resistance.

Her skin was the sweetest thing he'd ever tasted; he was ruined for desserts forever. His lips made a trail from her neck to her breast, and the gasps and moans she made as he closed his lips around her nipple bubbled in his veins like champagne. He sucked gently and swirled his tongue in a circle around the hardening bud as her fingers clamped onto his arms.

"Max," she moaned.

"I'm just getting started," he said against her skin. He licked his way over to the other nipple, repeating the treatment. By the time he moved further down, she was arching against him and gasping for breath. When he reached ribs that were more visible than he expected, he scraped his teeth gently across them, surprised by how much weight she had lost since they'd first met.

The stress she'd described a few minutes earlier had taken a harder toll on her than he'd initially realized. But he was a chef; if there was one thing in this world he was good at, it was feeding people. Nourishing them. He liked to think in both body and soul.

He chuckled against her skin, reminded of one of his first steps down the road that had led them here—it all came back to wanting to feed her.

And he would. Again. Soon. Later.

He wrapped his hand around her knee and raised his head to look up at her. "Can I move you?"

"God, Max, you can do anything you want to me," she whispered.

"Duly noted." He bent her knee and slid her leg up and over. "How about this?" He slid a finger gently along her crease, following it with his lips.

"Yes, yes, yes," she chanted.

"Mmm. And this?" He tasted her, finally, and her 'yes' turned into a shriek.

He grinned against her warmth and dove in, finding the perfect angle to swirl his tongue against her clit to make her shake. He kept one hand splayed against her hips and brought the other to her entrance, touching gently and waiting for her.

"Please," she whispered. "More."

He slid one finger into her, letting the flat of his tongue swipe against it as he took her higher. Her breathing grew faster, more labored, and she arched against his hand on her hip. He added pressure to keep her in one place and slid a second finger inside her, sucking gently on her clit and curving his fingers and tongue against her. He felt her stiffening a second before she came crying out his name. It was the best thing he'd heard all day. He stroked her through it until she went limp against him, then raised his head to look at her.

She met his eyes and smiled, dark and sultry, and

his own hips bucked against the edge of the bed helplessly.

"Come here," she said.

Obeying, he slid his body along hers, enjoying the shudders underneath him as he hit every sensitive part of her. He took it slow, and by the time he lay full against her, they were both gasping for air. She shifted, opened her legs wider, and he groaned as he felt his cock brush her warm, wet heat. "Nightstand," he said. "Hang on."

She nodded, and used the time it took him to reach with one arm into the drawer of his bedside table to reduce him to a quivering wreck by tracing the inside of his other elbow with her tongue and teeth.

"Oh, god. Lizzie ... ah ... let me—" Soon the words coming out of his mouth weren't even words at all, more like grunts and half-formed syllables, as he tore the condom open with shaking hands and somehow managed to get it rolled on. Then he moved over her, and suddenly her hands were everywhere, raking against him, tugging him downward, sliding over his ass. Her lips met his again, the sweetness of her mouth mixing with the deeper flavor of her core, and he thought he might actually come right then and there.

He slid a hand down between them and closed it around the base of his cock, willing himself to hold out. She chuckled, a low and dirty sound, as he buried his face in her skin, mouthing her neck and breasts and every inch he could reach. She did the same, and

the scrape of her teeth against his collarbone
undid him.

He rose up, shifted them both, and finally did what he'd been wanting to do since the first day she'd showed up on his doorstep.

Sinking into her felt like coming home.

12

*L*izzie shut off the light in the bathroom and slowly opened the door, cringing as its hinges squeaked in the hazy, post-dawn light. She paused in the doorway, admiring the view. Across the room, Max lay sprawled on his stomach in bed, the sheets pooled around his hips. The man had a truly excellent back. *And his backside isn't too bad either*, she thought to herself as she recalled anchoring her nails into his skin and pulling him deeper into her body.

Goodness, they'd been insatiable for one another. Lizzie wasn't a nun, but she'd never known sex could be like *that*. Hell, she'd never known *she* could be like that.

Everything about last night had been a revelation.

Normally, she was so focused on making sure her body was in the right position, or that she was doing something some magazine had recommended, that she'd often forget to enjoy herself. With Max, however, that hadn't been an issue. *At all.* If anything, she felt slightly guilty for the amount of effort he'd put into pleasing her instead of the other way around.

But not guilty enough to actually feel bad about it. She couldn't lie; being worshipped was a nice change of pace.

Quietly, she slipped back into the bedroom and tiptoed her way across the carpet to the warm cocoon of Max's bed. When she lifted the sheet to climb back in, he rolled onto his side and propped his head in his palm, his hair mussed and his lips tipped up in a happy smile.

"Good morning."

She settled in next to him. "Morning."

"I reached for you and you were gone."

"Sorry," she whispered, scooting closer. "Just sneaking off to the bathroom. Didn't want to subject you to my dragon breath."

"My very own Daenerys Targaryen." He tugged her body closer.

"Does that make you my Jon Snow?" she asked

playfully, setting her palm on his sternum and feeling his heart beating steady and strong beneath it.

He dropped a quick kiss onto her forehead and, without warning, swiftly rolled her onto her back. She squeaked, and he brushed a lock of blonde hair away from her face. "Despite it looking like Winterfell out there, no thank you. Dragon lady was hot, I'll give you that, but I still can't get past the whole Aunt Dany thing."

She chuckled and linked her arms around his neck, tangling her fingers in the thick, dark hair at his nape. "Is it weird for me to tell you how much I like this?"

His eyes danced over her face appreciatively. "Only if it's weird for me to say that I like *you*."

"I like you too," she whispered, her mood sobering slightly. Last night had been one of the most amazing nights of her life, but her happiness felt fleeting. Fragile.

With an uncertain future looming on the horizon, she didn't want to get too far ahead of herself by spinning fairy tales in her head of happily-ever-afters when she wasn't even sure she could give him a happily-ever-this-week. Still, after the intimacy they'd shared, she owed it him to be honest about her feelings.

But maybe not until tomorrow, she thought when he dropped his face forward to claim her mouth in a slow slide of lips and tongue that had her arching her back and panting for more. *Maybe we can just focus on today.*

WITH EACH FLICK of Max's wrist over the pan of portobello mushrooms, spinach, and eggs, his back muscles flexed, and Lizzie's mouth watered. Whether it was from the sight of the sexy man in black boxer briefs wearing an "I like pig butts and I cannot lie" apron, or the delicious smells filling his kitchen, she couldn't say. Maybe it was both. Either way, right now she was one *very* happy lady.

His phone chimed on the counter next to him, and he leaned over to check it. All morning, he'd been inundated with messages, mostly from his group of friends checking in with each other to make sure they'd made it through the night unscathed. Her phone had buzzed a few times, too, but not nearly as much as his.

Earlier, when Noah had asked how he'd ridden out the storm, Max's response had been brief and vague, something she was supremely thankful for. They hadn't had a chance to talk yet about what last night meant for their relationship, and until they did, she wasn't comfortable with his friends knowing she'd spent the night.

"That was Maeve," he said over his shoulder. "She's going to keep Mia until tomorrow morning. They haven't plowed her street yet and she doesn't want to risk driving until they do."

"Good idea." Maeve drove the tiniest car Lizzie had

ever seen. In fact, it was so small she wasn't sure it could even be classified as a car. It looked more like a go-kart, thus making it completely unsuited to drive in any sort of inclement weather. Not to mention that Mia was very precious cargo.

Max opened his mouth as if to say more, but then snapped it closed and turned his attention back to the omelet he was cooking for her. "I would have offered to pick her up myself, but I wasn't sure what your plans were for the day."

Lizzie glanced down at her bare legs tucked up into one of Max's Culinary Institute of America sweatshirts, a pair of thick hiking socks she'd borrowed from him dwarfing her much smaller feet, and then out his kitchen window. His yard was a shimmering sea of diamond white, with icicles hanging from the branches of his oak tree sparkling in the pale sunlight. Given that her car probably wasn't any better than Maeve's in these conditions, she'd assumed she'd be staying put a bit longer. Especially since her next door neighbor had let her know that the hill to their town-homes remained closed to traffic. No one was coming in or going out. If Max was trying to signal that he wanted her to hit the road, she honestly didn't know where she'd go.

"At the risk of sounding presumptuous, with all that snow—" she tilted her head toward the window "—I just figured we'd be stuck with each other a little longer." She tried to inject a note of humor in her voice. The type that said *Isn't it funny we had sex and now you can't get rid of me?*

He lifted his apron off over his head and tossed it onto the counter, then hoisted the sizzling pan from the fire and scooped the omelets onto a matching pair of white ceramic plates. He placed one down in front of her, then settled into the empty chair across from her with the other.

"If I had things my way, I'd be stuck here with you clear into next week." He winked, and scooped a forkful of eggs into his mouth.

She smiled back at him, knowing it hadn't quite reached her eyes. The idea of being cooped up with Max for several days made her stomach flutter in a way she'd never experienced before. She thought the sensation was mostly positive, but a little voice at the back of her head also warned her that falling for him could prove risky. For months they'd been dancing around their attraction to one another, ignoring the certain … something … that was brewing between them. In the span of a days they'd gone from something that resembled friends into … whatever this was. They probably needed to talk about that. Figure out what their night together meant in the grand scheme of things.

It wasn't a conversation she was particularly looking forward to, but it was one they needed to have. They'd crossed a line yesterday—and then again last night and early this morning—that had drastically changed their dynamic. Aside from that, her life was in a period of serious upheaval, and as much as she wanted to be with Max, she had a lot to figure out before she could commit to a relationship with him.

To a relationship with Mia, too, when it came right down to it. The girl might not be Max's biological child, but he was effectively a single dad now, and any woman he brought into his life would need to understand that he was a package deal. Full guardianship would come through any day now, solidifying their little family unit. Lizzie didn't want to be a third wheel to their pair, or be the woman who came between them. She'd seen it more times than she cared to remember, and even if she went into this thing with eyes wide open, she knew it could still happen.

"About that ..." she said.

He set his fork to the side and slid his hand across the table, settling it atop hers. "I can see the wheels turning in your brain. Did I say or do something wrong?"

She dropped her eyes down to her plate, unable to meet his penetrating gaze, and chewed on her lip as she tried to formulate her thoughts. "No, not wrong per se ... just, well ... you've got me thinking. I came here yesterday on a whim. I didn't really intend for any of this to happen." She raised her eyes back up to meet his. "In fact, I'd promised myself it *wouldn't*. But then I quit, and ... well. You know what happened next."

"I do. And for the record, it was everything I hoped

for. No," he said with a quick shake of his head. "It was more. You're *more*, Lizzie."

"Maaaaax ..." she drew his name out as one long syllable. She felt exactly the same way, but she was trying to be realistic, too. This wasn't some dalliance they could walk away from when one of them tired of the other. There was a very special little girl to think of involved in all of this, and Lizzie wouldn't risk Mia's happiness—even if it meant ignoring her own.

He squeezed her hand. "Can I ask you for a favor?"

"Yes, of course."

His eyes bounced to the snowy yard then back to her. "Today, it's just you and me, snowed in with nowhere else to be. No other responsibilities to think about. I'm not an idiot; I know the second the snow melts and Mia comes bouncing through the front door, this all changes. I'll go back to being a new parent, and you'll go back to dealing with your job situation. We'll each go back to putting everyone else's wants and needs in front of our own. So today, just for this short while, will you be a little selfish with me? Will you take the day to just enjoy ourselves? Enjoy what we have together?"

She stared at him for a few beats, letting his words settle in her mind. In her heart. She'd arrived at his house a woman on a mission, while he'd been the one trying to slow that train down. But then he'd capitulated, and ever since then it was like he'd decided to stop fighting his feelings, to embrace them fully. While in a perfect world that would have been everything she wanted, they didn't live in a perfect world, and she'd begun to worry she was going to have to be the one to put a cork in their little world of wintry make believe. Max understanding that this thing between them might only be temporary should have put her mind at ease. Unfortunately, it didn't.

She wasn't sure her mind would ever be at ease again.

Which was all the more reason for her to do what he asked. To be a little bit selfish with him, for just a little while. To take hold of the limited time they had together and make the most of it.

She nodded. "Yeah, I can do that."

He smiled at her then, that wide, honest grin that made her insides feel all gooey and warm. "Good, now come here." He slid his chair back, the legs scraping against the slate tile, and patted his thigh.

Suddenly, she wasn't hungry anymore. Well, at least not for her omelet. She wanted to get her mouth around something much more satisfying.

Obediently, Lizzie stood from her chair and made her way around the table to him, straddling his lap and sinking down to settle herself against the bulge growing hard and thick beneath the black cotton covering him.

When he groaned, she giggled. "Do you remember when you were texting me about your sausage?" she asked apropos of nothing as she scraped her fingernails through the dark hair on his chest.

"Yeah, I remember," he answered, his low, gravelly voice causing her to shiver. The way Max sounded when he was turned on might be the sexiest thing she'd ever heard.

"I have a confession."

"Oh yeah?"

She nodded. "For a minute there, I thought you might not be talking *about* actual sausage. It wasn't until I picked Mia up at the restaurant and you handed me that container that I realized you weren't subliminally talking about this." She rolled her pelvis against him, her meaning clear.

He chuckled. "This? You're going to have to be more specific, sweetheart."

Lizzie cast him an exasperated look. She wasn't a person given to dirty talk, but apparently when she had a sexy man encouraging her, she was prone to say all sorts of things she'd never uttered before. Things like "Fuck me, Max," and "Oh god, your dick is so fucking beautiful."

But that had been last night. When it was dark, and they were in bed.

Now, they were sitting in his kitchen in the bright light of day, his hard cock pulsing between her thighs. As much as she wanted to let loose that new-found side of her, she didn't know if she could bring herself to actually say such filthy things to him here. Now. Didn't know if she could be the type of woman who told a man exactly how she wanted him and where.

"Max."

"Lizzie …" he drawled, a mischievous twinkle sparkling in his garnet-flecked eye. "Say it if you want to."

She did want to, it turned out. "Your dick, okay?" she laughed, loving how free she could be with him. "I thought sausage was a euphemism for your dick."

His lips tipped to the side in a smirk. "Wanna know a secret?"

She nodded her head emphatically. Ever since she was a little girl, Lizzie had *loved* secrets. It didn't matter how big or small, she coveted them. And once shared, she never told a soul. It was a trait that made her so good at her job. People instinctively knew they could trust her with their innermost thoughts. And right now, she wanted to know all of Max's.

"Yes, please. Gimme." She made grabby hands at him, and he smiled at her with adoration for a brief moment before his grin turned positively feral.

"You were right," he said, his voice a strange mixture of lust and humor that was so uniquely him. "I *was* talking about my dick, but when I realized I'd been less than subtle about it, I panicked. Luckily I had all the ingredients available in the walk-in. I've never whipped up a batch that quickly in my life." By the time he was done talking, his chest was bouncing with laughter, his abs flexing into sharp ridges.

Lizzie smacked his chest playfully. "I knew it!"

He swiped at his eyes. "You had me pegged all along."

Something about knowing her unbridled lust hadn't been one sided was supremely satisfying. Knowing that he'd been thinking about fucking her while sending her seemingly innocuous texts made her pulse race. Made her even more cognizant of the hard pressure pressed against her core.

Lizzie wasn't a woman prone to having sex in the middle of the afternoon. In a kitchen. She didn't reach down, pull a man's cock out of his underwear, and squeeze it between shaking fingers. She wasn't someone who pushed up onto her toes, hooked her underwear to the side, and rubbed that cock against her slick, swollen entrance.

She wasn't a woman who did any of this. And yet with Max, maybe she was.

"Do *you* wanna know a secret?" she asked, mimicking his earlier question while batting her eyelashes coquettishly.

"Yeah," he grunted, pupils blown black with desire.

She leaned forward, her slick body teasing him with the movement. "I'll always want your sausage," she whispered huskily into his ear as she rolled her hips over him for added emphasis.

He gripped them roughly to still her movement. "You're dangerous."

She leaned back and shrugged playfully. "Who knew?"

He chuckled, dark and low. "Oh, I knew, all right."

"Max?" she breathed.

"Yeah?"

"Take me to bed."

Abruptly, he pushed up from his chair, hoisting her up with him, and she wound her legs around his waist and twined her arms around his neck. In no time at all, they were down his hallway and stumbling into his bedroom. Soon, she was on her back and he was rolling a condom down his length. And then she was parting her legs and he was pressing against her.

"And I'll always want you."

And then he was in her, and she was screaming his name.

13

Twenty-four hours with Lizzie naked in his bed wasn't nearly enough, but it was all he was going to get. Just a few selfish moments in between bouts of homework, heated discussions with farmers over their wilted produce deliveries, and interviews with new servers. And yet, limited though their time together had been, he didn't regret a single second of it. In fact, as he opened the front door for her and tucked her scarf firmly into the collar of her coat, he let his fingers linger on her shoulders for a few minutes, wondering if he should have asked for more.

She smiled up at him. "Ready to take on the

future?" she asked, and he felt it like a punch in the stomach. *The future.* That uncertain, nebulous thing hanging over their heads. The reason he hadn't asked for more than just a day with her.

"You know it," he said, pasting on his best grin and leaning in for one last kiss. He had to make it count.

"Mmm." She pulled away before his hand could slide under her coat and settle against her hip. "If you keep doing that, I'll never get out the door."

Sounds good to me, he thought. But the plows had finally come through, and Maeve would be here with Mia soon. There was schoolwork to organize, lunch to make, and work to do. He let Lizzie go. "See you soon?"

She shrugged, not quite meeting his eyes. "Hope so." They hadn't ever quite managed to have the 'what's next?' talk. And he wouldn't push her. Couldn't push himself, either. She had a job hunt to undertake, and he had a kid who needed him and a restaurant to run.

"Yeah. Me too." He realized there was nothing else to say, so he watched her carefully pick her way through snow and ice down to her car, and potentially out of his life. He waved her off, keeping an eye on her vehicle as it navigated the narrowly-plowed street until she turned the corner at the end of the road and disappeared. Suddenly, he realized how cold he was out here on his stoop. "Shit." He wasn't even wearing shoes.

He slammed the door closed and went to check his phone. Mia's school had sent an automated texted to alert everyone they would be closed again today, but he didn't have the luxury of keeping Frankie's closed. If he and enough of his staff could get in, they'd open up right on time and start feeding the citizens of River Hill, many of whom were still without electricity and would need to seek sustenance elsewhere. He found a notepad and scratched a few notes. They could easily add a quick chili to the menu for both lunch and dinner. Maybe something with potatoes, too. He'd need to start making calls to vendors as soon as he got in to check who'd been able to save what. *What a mess.*

The faint scrape of tires against packed snow let him know that Mia and Maeve had arrived. He opened the door for his niece, waved to Maeve to let her know she could stay in her warm car, and let reality settle back over him. His wintry interlude with Lizzie was over.

The rest of the day, predictably, was pure chaos. He took Mia to the restaurant with him, tucked her in a corner with her homework, and got to work. Customers started pouring in by noon, and the rush never ended. Wendy ruled the kitchen with an iron fist while he helped out anywhere and everywhere he could; racing out to pick up an extra case of root vegetables a local farmer offered at a discount given the frost, picking up service at a table here and there, and doing time behind the bar.

He even managed to help Mia with a math problem on his way to wipe down the booth behind her, although when she asked him for help with another one further down the page he threw up his hands in despair and yelled for one of the waitresses who was in college to come help her. "Turns out middle school math is too hard for me," he said as he traded his dishcloth for her apron. "I'll grab table eleven for you."

He didn't see most of his friends all day, since they had their own businesses to take care of. He assumed Sean was as busy as he was across the square at The Breadery, and Jess was probably helping out. Angelica and Noah had texted yesterday that they expected to get The Oakwell's long drive plowed this morning, and then spend all day over in the vineyard with his crew assessing the grapes. Maeve and Ben volunteered for several organizations in town, so they were probably being good citizens and helping out somewhere. Iain and Naomi hadn't responded to any group texts after she'd sent one that was just the fire emoji followed immediately by the eggplant one, so he assumed they were holed up in their house like he and Lizzie had been earlier. Only, of course, they got to stay that way.

Eventually, however, the gang all trickled in toward the end of the dinner rush. Noah and Angelica were first, looking wiped out and wet from tramping through icy, wet grapevines all day. Maeve and Ben followed, looking as annoyingly perky as they always did, and Noah grumbled at them over his beer. "Can't you two at least look tired?"

"We just get so many endorphins from helping people, Noah," Ben responded with a shit-eating grin. God, he was cocky.

"Endorphins, my ass," Angelica moaned. "She's ten years younger than I am, and you spend every free hour you have at the gym." She draped herself dramatically across the bar. "Give me something deeply alcoholic, Max."

Max laughed. "We mulled some cider this morning, and I've got just enough left for a large mug. Want me to spike it?"

"Hard. Spike it hard."

He drew some cider out of the carafe on the back counter and added bourbon to it before handing it over. "Drown your woes." He glanced at Noah. "Speaking of woes, how did it go?"

The big man let go of his beer long enough to scrape a hand over his face, against the dark stubble that had grown in. Max suspected his own face was equally scruffy; why was it that facial hair seemed to grow faster when you were tired? "It's actually not too bad. We didn't anticipate actual snow, but the vines are dormant for winter. It was mostly a matter of checking on things and hauling out a bunch of downed limbs from various trees."

"If I never see another tree pruner I'll be a happy woman," Angelica chimed in, lifting her palms to show off a row of blisters.

"We did the same thing over at the community

garden," Maeve said. "After we fed puppies at the shelter."

"Don't say the P-word," Max hissed. "She might hear you." He jerked his head toward Mia, who was sucking down a milkshake that Wendy had inexplicably made her while she read what appeared to be a graphic novel.

Maeve grinned at him. "When you're ready, I'll help you pick one out."

"I will never be ready."

Jess and Sean saved him from defending his no-puppy policy by showing up with Iain and Naomi in tow, all four of them blowing through the door with a gust of chill wind as Iain held it open for another customer departing.

"How'd you get the hermits out?" Max asked Sean when they got to the bar, nodding his head at Naomi, who looked annoyed.

"He promised me apple fritters," Naomi said, pointing at Iain with an air of deep disgust.

The Irish man put his hands up in self defense. "How was I to know they'd be out?"

"You could have called ahead," Jess said mildly.

"You could have called ahead!" Naomi repeated. "See?"

"Oh, don't act like you thought of that until just now," Iain teased her. "You could have done it, too."

"Nooooo," she said slowly, as though he were a small child. "I was to be the beneficiary of said fritters.

Nobel Prize winners don't call up and make sure the medal's ready before they head over to Switzerland. That's the person handing them the medal's job!"

"Did you just compare my apple fritters to the Nobel Prize?" Sean asked. "Not to mention, you two showed up right after we closed."

Naomi flapped her hand at him. "Take the compliment and don't sweat the details, baker boy."

Jess laughed. "Maybe we can put it on your advertising, honey." She curved her hand over her still-flat belly as she hopped up onto a bar stool. "Fritters so good they're like the Nobel."

"We'll workshop it," Sean answered, scooting in behind her to wrap his arms around her and drop a kiss on her head.

Max watched them for a moment, resolutely ignoring the twinge of jealousy low in his gut, before turning away to gather food and drinks for his friends. There was too much to do right now for him to think about how Sean and Jess revolved around each other in easy harmony, or how Iain and Naomi's friendly sparring led to them huddled together, low-voiced and kissing breathlessly like they hadn't just spent the day together in bed. Or the way Noah and Angelica had come in together after spending hours in the least sexy way imaginable, still loving each other because they were partners and friends.

It filled him with happiness to see his friends so settled. It also made him think things he wasn't supposed to be thinking. He gritted his teeth as he handed Maeve her bowl of chili and slid a plate of tacos toward Ben as he inwardly vowed to let it go.

But of course his friends weren't going to let him. Angelica, curse her, only gave him enough time to get everybody settled in before she focused that laser glare on him. "Where's Lizzie? I haven't heard from her all day."

He shrugged. "At home, I guess."

That was apparently the wrong thing to say. Her eyes narrowed, and now Maeve was looking at him strangely, too.

But it was Ben who said something, damn him. "You guess? You don't know?"

Max's fingers tightened around the edge of the bar involuntarily. He looked down and saw that his knuckles were white. "Not for sure, no." He focused on loosening his fingers, one by one.

"Did something happen, Max?" Jess spoke softly.

His hands were free of the bar top, finally, so he ran one through his hair, remembering her hands doing the same hours earlier. "She, ah, quit her job. So I guess we'll be getting a new caseworker." They hadn't talked about that either, actually. He perked up, realizing that he actually had a real reason to contact her. "I'm not sure of the details, but I'll find out soon."

"Is that it?" Angelica was a bloodhound on the scent.

He shot her a glare. "Yes. That's it." That was all he

was going to say about it, anyway. Especially with Mia just a few feet away. He tried to communicate that with only his eyebrows, but he wasn't sure it went through. Angelica's lips thinned, but she didn't press him any further about it.

Before anyone could bring it up again, he decided to make a hasty retreat. "I'm going to have to take Mia home," he told his friends. "Stay until close, if you want."

"Oh, we will," Ben said with a laugh. He twined his fingers with Maeve's, and Max tore his eyes away before he could resent his best friend even more.

But as the week rolled on, he found himself thinking about that day more and more. Yes, he'd spent twenty-four glorious hours on top of, under, inside, and around Lizzie Teague in multiple ways both nude and semi-clothed and once, memorably, tied up. But he'd also cooked for her, and talked to her about topics ranging from TV shows to gardening techniques, and spent time simply laying with her watching the snow fall outside his living room window.

And he'd enjoyed it all nearly as much as the sex.

He hadn't been lying when he'd told Lizzie at the New Year's Eve party that he missed her friendship. Spending time with her had been one of the highlights of the last few months, and he was desperately afraid that he'd made a huge mistake when he'd told her he didn't mind her walking out the door.

Eventually, he received an email from the Department of Social Services, then another one from the new caseworker assigned to Mia. Everything was on track with his guardianship, and there would only be one more home visit before everything was signed off on in March. He typed and deleted a text to Lizzie about it twice, then didn't send anything at all.

His friends weren't helping matters either. They were all blissfully domestic, and he kept seeing himself and Lizzie in his imagination every time he ran into Sean and Jess jogging together, or witnessed Noah and Angelica bent over a wedding magazine. Ben sent him texts that were increasingly short and to the point about getting his shit together, and Max mostly sent middle finger emojis back.

The problem was, his shit *was* together. He wanted Lizzie. But he also wanted to be the parent Mia needed, and the restauranteur all those investors who kept emailing seemed to think he was. And Lizzie was on the cusp of something amazing, he was sure of it. On to bigger and better things, helping people the way she'd dreamed of. She might not realize yet that her explosive exit from her job had been the right move, but he knew *her*, and he firmly believed that she was destined for something amazing. It wasn't a matter of *if* she found it; only when.

How could he ask her to give up the future that she'd just blown wide open when he had so little to give her in return?

14

izzie was a Hufflepuff. At least according to the "Which Harry Potter House Are You?" quiz she'd just taken. At first, she took umbrage with the designation, but the more she considered it, the less offended she became. Hufflepuffs were known to be creative, patient, and loyal—traits she possessed in spades.

But how did these qualities translate to a new career? She'd sat down to apply for jobs, but instead wound up analyzing her future, and the only thing she'd come up with to help her decide was online personality quizzes. There had to be a way to take everything she'd learned these past few years and apply it to something that didn't have her pushing papers or driving all over kingdom come for suited bureaucrats who only cared about their bottom line instead of the people they were supposed to be helping. As far as she could tell, no office within a one-hundred-mile radius was in any better position than the one she'd just left. If she wanted to do something meaningful with her life, she was going to have to formulate a new game plan.

Just as soon as she found out what her favorite food revealed about her taste in men.

IT HAD BEEN four days since Lizzie left Max's house and set out to find herself. Ninety-six long hours in which she'd picked up the phone about a million and one times to ask his advice about her career. She hadn't intended to ghost him, but the longer they went without speaking, the easier it was to tell herself that she was doing the right thing. Their night together had been the stuff dreams were made of, but that was just it: they were dreaming if they thought they could ever be anything more.

And yet a small voice at the back of her head kept asking why. *Why can't you be with him? Why can't you make this work? Why, why, why?*

And over and over again, she came back to the

same answer: "Because it's wrong. He's my client." But that wasn't true anymore, either.

So if he *wasn't* her client, and she wasn't Mia's caseworker, what exactly were they? The ethics of hooking up with him were still murky given that she needed to retain her license to practice social work if she wanted to find a new job, so until she could see a clear path forward, she decided it was best to stay away altogether.

"You're avoiding us." Angelica stood on Lizzie's front porch with her arms crossed over her chest, her toe tapping the bricks at her high-heeled feet.

Lizzie unlatched the screen door and pushed it open. "I'm not avoiding you," she said, stepping aside to allow Angelica to enter. She pointed toward the coat rack in the corner of the foyer and then stood there awkwardly, unsure what to say as the curvy vixen divested herself of her scarf and winter coat.

"I've texted you twice, and you missed book club."

"I—" Lizzie closed her mouth around the denial she was about to issue. There was no use arguing; she *was* avoiding them. She let out a sigh. "Have you had coffee yet?"

"Two cups. But I need at least three to get going in the morning. Lead the way."

"Come on then." She gestured toward the kitchen, and Angelica followed closely behind.

"Cute place."

"I like it."

"How long have you lived here?"

Lizzie reached into the tall cupboard that housed her Nespresso capsules, and set the machine to brew a double shot of espresso. "Seven years. I bought it after renting a small one bedroom that was really just a garage in someone's back yard. And before you say it," Lizzie added as she passed Angelica her coffee, "I'm aware that Max has an apartment over his garage."

The existence of unexpected garage apartments in their lives was something she and Max had first bonded over. While they were still in that awkward 'I don't really know you but I'm spending a lot of time in your house' phase of their association, she'd kept a running tally of all the little things she could get him to talk about. One night, she'd spied him coming down the lamp-lit staircase above his garage before coming inside to take over child care duties for the night. Curious, she'd asked him about it, and he'd explained he had a small apartment up there that both Iain and Ben had lived in when they'd first arrived in River Hill. At first she'd been surprised, but the more she got to know him, the more it made sense. Whether he realized it about himself or not, Max was a nurturer. If his friends or the community needed him, he'd find a way to be there for them.

"I wasn't going to say anything," Angelica demurred over the rim of her cup, her eyes twinkling with mischief. "But now that you mention it, have you talked to him lately?"

Lizzie joined her at the small round table. "No. Not since the storm."

Angelica nodded. "So many people are complaining about how horrible it was, but I kind of enjoyed it. There's something really magical about being trapped inside with a handsome man while the world comes to an icy standstill all around you. You'd know that if you'd have come to last week's meeting. Which reminds me, how'd *you* weather the storm?" Angelica's face was a mask of innocence, which meant she knew perfectly well where Lizzie had been. She was a good actress, but she had a terrible poker face.

"He told you."

Angelica laughed, and set her empty cup to the side. "No, but you just did."

"Damn it." Lizzie's mug joined Angelica's. "Does anyone else know?"

"Maybe? Probably? Maeve mentioned there was a second set of tire tracks in his driveway when she dropped Mia off, but he was cagey about it when she asked him."

"A regular Nancy Drew," Lizzie mused. She hadn't even thought of that as she'd pulled away. She'd been too busy alternating between congratulating herself for having ended her dry spell with the sexiest man she'd ever met and castigating herself over the fact that in doing so she'd crossed a huge line. And she hadn't stopped since then. Frankly, she was developing a case of whiplash as often as she went back and forth.

"Maeve's protective of Max, so she sees things about him others might not," Angelica answered.

That sounded … not ideal. "He and Maeve haven't … you know?"

Angelica waved away her suspicions. "Oh god, no. They're more like brother and sister than anything. It's kind of adorable, actually. Max hasn't had a serious girlfriend since I've been here, and since Maeve was single when *she* moved out here, I thought about playing matchmaker, but it was obvious they'd never be anything more than really good friends. With the rest of us coupled up, they kind of formed their own little coalition."

"That's … interesting." Of everything she and Max had discussed these last few months, they'd studiously avoided their romantic histories. There'd really never been a reason *to* discuss it, and yet she couldn't deny she'd often wondered. A man like him was a catch with a capital C. Why *hadn't* he had a girlfriend?

"I can see the question in your eyes," Angelica continued, her ability to guess Lizzie's thoughts disconcerting. "It's not my story to tell, but I will say this: Max guards his heart very closely, but I've never seen him look at anyone the way he looks at you." With that, she pushed her chair back and stood, raising her wrist up to look at her watch. "Sorry I have to chat and run, but I'm meeting with the wedding florist in forty-five minutes and I want to beat traffic."

Dazed, Lizzie accompanied her to the door. "I'm sorry," she said when Angelica had donned her jacket once again. "I didn't mean to shut you out. Things are ... complicated."

"Of course they are. If love was easy, it would be far less rewarding, don't you think?"

"Oh, we're not—"

Angelica smiled, and patted Lizzie's arm as if to say *You keep on telling yourself that*. Then she opened the door and stepped out onto the stoop. Before striding down the walk—there was really no other way to describe the way Angelica moved through life—she turned back to Lizzie. "And by the way. We like you for *you*; not just because you're Max's ... whatever. Don't be a stranger, okay?"

Bowled over by this unequivocal declaration of friendship, Lizzie found her head bobbing up and down in agreement. "Yeah, okay." She didn't know if she had any intention of honoring the commitment, but it was nice to know that she was wanted.

Maggie sent over another page of job listings, and by some small miracle one of them sounded right up Lizzie's alley. Assuming, of course, she was willing to relocate to Miami. She liked the beach, but the humidity? Not so much. And hurricanes? Definitely not. Still, it was a job. And a well-paying one at that. So before she could talk herself out of it, she typed out a short letter listing all the reasons why they should consider her for the position, attached her resume, and hit send.

LIZZIE STARED at Patterson University's website. It'd been two days since a random internet quiz had revealed she should be a therapist, and she hadn't stopped thinking about the possibilities since. She'd written a few papers in college about therapeutic techniques, and she'd really enjoyed the pilot wellness program she and Maggie had run, but generally speaking, she'd always thought of herself as a caseworker, not a counselor.

Last night she'd stayed up late again poring over articles on the various types of therapy that were explicitly geared toward children. Through a stroke of good luck—and really excellent Facebook stalking skills—she discovered that a former classmate ran a practice focused solely on child play therapy. From the way it was described on her website, it sounded incredible. It wound up being the inspiration Lizzie desperately needed to guide her way forward. She finally felt like there was something she really wanted to do with her life.

The problem was, while she had many of the qualifications one needed to pursue a position as a play therapist, she was lacking a Master's degree in counseling. She was a licensed social worker—an LCSW, not an LCPC, a licensed clinical professional counselor— and the degree made a major difference in what she could do.

It had been a long time since Lizzie was in school, and she was scared to think what it would be like going back at the ripe old age of thirty-four. But starting a new job in a city she'd never lived in before was just as frightening a prospect, and choosing between moving to Miami to do the same thing that had been burning her out (assuming she even got an interview) versus pursuing this new, rewarding dream seemed like a nobrainer. If she was going to do something scary either way, why not pursue the one that fed her soul?

So, just as she'd done a few days before, Lizzie filled out an application and put together a letter that explained who she was, why she was interested in the program, and how her professional experience was applicable, and then hit send before she could talk herself out of it.

LIZZIE SCROLLED THROUGH HER DVR, searching for something interesting to watch. She'd been officially unemployed for a couple of weeks, and she was well past the point of boredom. The longest vacation she'd ever taken was a four-night trip down to Mexico for her uncles' joint birthday celebration, and even then she'd been anxious to get back to work.

Since her savings would take her through a few more months without a job, she'd been scrupulous about the opportunities she'd applied to. Now it was just a matter of waiting and seeing. And waiting some more.

With so much free time on her hands, she was at a loss for how to fill it. So far, she'd tried the whole spa day thing, but she'd been way too tense to enjoy the massage. And as she'd promised, she'd met up with Angelica for coffee, although not in River Hill where she might run into Max.

Not that avoiding him kept her from thinking about him.

While she'd hoped her desire to speak with him about what was going on in her life would wane the longer they were apart, the exact opposite was true. How many times had she been tempted to send him one of the dozens of online quizzes she'd taken so she could learn what mythical creature he was, or what his favorite coffee drink said about his personality?

And it wasn't like she found any respite from the constant yearning for him when she fell asleep. If anything, the dreams might be worse. No matter what topic her mind latched onto at night, visions of Max somehow permeated her dreams. Things had gotten so bad that she'd woken up at three o'clock this morning —shaking and pulsing—his name on her lips as she came to visions of his face between her legs.

Discovering that she'd depleted her cache of go-to TV shows, Lizzie tossed the remote to the side and reached for her laptop. She opened up her browser and was midway through typing in the address for what was fast becoming her favorite celebrity gossip website when her phone rang. She glanced around to find it, eventually pulling it out from underneath a cushion, and her breath caught when she saw the name on the caller ID.

When she'd first become Mia's caseworker, she'd programmed every possible number to reach both Vergarases into her phone—including the land line Max said he never used and was thinking of doing away with. Since Mia was too young to have a cell phone, Lizzie had encouraged him to keep it for the girl's sake. There was no reason for Max to call her from it, so that meant it must be his niece. But why? If something was wrong with him, wouldn't Angelica or someone have told her already?

As quickly as the question came to her, she tossed it aside. The answer was no. She wasn't Mia's case-worker anymore, and she certainly wasn't Max's girl-friend. At this point, she wasn't even sure she could say they were friends.

So why was a nine-year-old reaching out to her out of the blue? Honestly, she was scared to find out. If something *had* happened, she wasn't sure she'd ever forgive herself.

With shaking fingers, she hit the button to accept the call. "Hello?"

"Lizzie?"

"I'm here, Mia. What's wrong?"

Please let Max be okay. Please let Max be okay. Please let Max be okay.

"I need your help."

Lizzie sat up straighter, her pulse pounding in her head. "Anything. Tell me."

The little girl's breath hitched, and then her voice dropped to a whisper. "The nuns at school said I need to go bra shopping."

All the blood rushed from Lizzie's head in a single *woosh*, and she found herself growing lightheaded. "What?"

Mia hiccuped and Lizzie realized she was crying. "Sister Agnes said I'm indecent, and I can't participate in recess or sports until I wear a bra."

Lizzie was ... horrified. Mia was only nine years old! Yes, she was a little more well developed than some of her peers, but there was nothing *indecent* at all about her. Sister Agnes, however, was a different story. Lizzie was ready to march straight into St. Aloysius and give the woman a piece of her mind.

Except ... that wasn't her place anymore.

So even though it went against every instinct she had, she took a deep breath and approached this conversation with reserved calmness. "What did your uncle say?"

She was back to whispering. "He doesn't know. I'm scared to tell him."

Scared? That didn't sound like the appropriate response, from either her clinical or personal perspective. Max was the furthest thing from scary that she could think of. "Why?"

"Because he's a *boy*, Lizzie."

Aha. Lizzie fought a smile. What a perfectly reasonable thing for a nine-year-old girl to think. "That's true," she conceded. "But he's also your guardian, and these are the types of things you two are going to encounter as you mature."

Mia sighed. "Maybe he'll get married, and I'll have an aunt who can talk to me about this stuff instead."

Those words, spoken so innocently, were like a punch to the gut. Lizzie had to clamp her mouth tightly shut to keep the sound of her pained gasp from reaching through the phone and alerting the girl to her distress. She pulled a breath in through her nose and forced herself to calm down. Mia could never know how much Lizzie was affected by the idea of Max meeting someone else. Eventually settling down with her. Growing their family.

"Maybe you can ask Naomi," she offered, proud when her voice didn't betray her chaotic emotions.

Mia snorted. "Naomi doesn't wear a bra."

"Angelica?"

"Liiiizzie," Mia whined. "Angelica's boobs are huge."

The kid wasn't wrong, but why that made the actress a bad choice for bra shopping was anyone's guess. If anything, it made her a perfect candidate. "Which means she knows a thing or two about bras, don't you think?"

"Yeah, *lacy* ones," Mia shot back quickly, as if the style and fabric of Angelica's bras was the most obvious thing in the world. "She's *very* fancy. I don't want to be fancy. That's why I called you."

Lizzie found herself smiling despite herself, and chose to take Mia's backhanded compliment in the spirit with which it was no doubt intended. She might not be Mia's caseworker any longer, but she still cared enormously for the girl. If she needed Lizzie's support with this, that's what she'd get. "Okay, I'll call your uncle and arrange to pick you up in an hour. How does Kohl's and In-n-Out sound?"

Mia squealed. "Yes! Oh my god. Thank you so much, Lizzie. You're the best."

When Mia hung up the phone, Lizzie sat on her sofa for a few minutes to catch her breath and prepare herself for the coming conversation. Once she mostly had control of her emotions, she pushed up off the sofa, dialed Max's number, and brought the phone to her ear.

"Hey, Max. It's Lizzie."

15

How had he gotten here, exactly? Max parked his Land Rover in front of the department store with a sense of vague confusion. He unlocked the doors and Mia and Lizzie hopped out, chattering together, while he went over the course of events in his mind.

Seeing Lizzie's name flashing on his caller ID, he'd picked up the phone with a surge of relief he didn't really want to examine too closely, only to discover she was calling about Mia. His heart had plummeted as quickly as it had soared, and for a moment he thought he might actually pass out. The swirl of his body's reactions had resolved itself into a burning sense of rage after Lizzie related what Mia had told her about Sister Agnes, coupled with a familiar sinking sense of failure and shame. Why hadn't Mia hadn't come to him about the comment from the nun?

Lizzie had reassured him it was totally normal for a nine-year-old girl to want to go to a female authority figure in this circumstance, but while he might understand it intellectually, somewhere inside of him everything was getting tangled up. Memories of Isabel drifting away from him as she'd become a teenager—her deep-seated resentment and lashing out after their parents had died while he'd tried his best to support and understand her, only to fail miserably—were clawing their way up from where he'd tried to bury them. Sometimes it felt like he'd failed his sister long before she died.

They were so fundamentally different that he'd been at an utter loss how to help her when she'd drifted, without ambition, from gig to gig and wherever her whims took her. When she'd told him she was pregnant at twenty-three, it had been so long since they'd tried to understand each other that he hadn't really known how to react. He'd asked if she needed money to take care of it, which had been entirely the wrong thing to say. She'd brushed him off, and the next time he heard from her she was on the road again with a new baby in tow.

With his memories of Isabel jumbled together with his worry for Mia, he'd somehow found himself standing in his driveway saying he'd come along on their shopping expedition—if his niece would allow it. He'd glanced at Lizzie, waiting for her to shut him down, but she'd quirked her lips in a strange little smile and said, "Whatever Mia wants. It's your money, after all."

Initially, he'd planned to hand over his credit card and go over to Ben's office to review some of the franchise offers he'd received, an activity that was long overdue if he wanted to keep moving forward with the idea. But instead, he'd piled the three of them into his car and now here they were.

Lizzie slowed down to let him catch up to her, while Mia dashed ahead to the automatic doors and jumped in front of them to make them open. "You sure about this?" she asked quietly.

He glanced over at her. She was red-cheeked from a chill breeze that was blowing her hair away from her face, her neck tucked down into the collar of her jacket, while she grinned fondly at Mia in the not-too-far distance. He'd never seen Lizzie look more beautiful, even when he'd been the one to put the flush in her cheeks on their memorable day together.

Which she hadn't brought up when she'd called him. He ought to be grateful that Lizzie loved his niece enough to help her out like this. He was. Honestly. But he also desperately wanted to discuss it. Now wasn't the time, though.

"How bad could it be?" he asked instead.

She visibly restrained her laughter. "Have you ever gone bra shopping before?"

"Uh." He swallowed. "Not … like this?"

She raised her eyebrows, clearly surprised by his answer, and he found his own cheeks heating as they entered the store. "I've, you know, been to Victoria's Secret. And stuff."

Her eyebrows went back down. "For your sister?"

"God, no." He had no idea who had taken Isabel bra shopping, actually. Their parents had still been alive when she was Mia's age, so it must have been their mother. Later, when she was a teenager, it might have been Ben's mom. It had never occurred to him to ask. Another thing he owed the Worthingtons. He'd long ago paid back the money that Ben had lent him to buy out the previous owner of Frankie's, but his debt to the whole family was something he'd never be able to repay. Not that they'd want him to.

As for Lizzie's question … friends, lovers, or something yet to be defined, he had to tell her about Vanessa. "I had a serious relationship several years ago."

"How serious?" She waved Mia to the left as they noticed that she'd been distracted by a display of charm bracelets. "Not our main objective today, kiddo."

He blew out a breath. He hated talking about this. "I had a ring."

She stopped dead and stared at him. "You did?"

He took her elbow and got her moving again, not particularly wanting Mia to come back over to investigate why they'd slowed down. "Yeah."

"What happened?"

He shrugged. "She left." God, he hated bringing this up. "I was too busy for her, I think."

Lizzie actually snorted. "God forbid you spend time running a successful restaurant." She shook her head. "She was an idiot."

Something warmed in the pit of his belly, and he smiled at her. "Thanks. I hear she's pretty happy now, so I guess it turned out okay." In more ways than one. Vanessa wouldn't have gotten along with his niece at all, he realized.

Lizzie was still shaking her head as they caught up to Mia, who was standing near the undergarments section of the store and looking entirely lost. Max glanced around, noticing they were surrounded by cups and bands and lacy bits in sensible beiges and bright jewel toned colors. He swallowed, and his eyes found Mia's. . He was pretty sure the look on his face was identical to hers, and the humor sparkling in Lizzie's eyes confirmed his hunch.

"Want to stay out here on the pathway where it's safe?" she asked, gesturing to the wide strip of linoleum they stood on.

He took a deep breath. "I need to know this stuff, right?" He pointed at Mia. "Your boobs aren't going anywhere."

She turned bright red. "Uncle MAX!"

Lizzie giggled. "Come on, Mia. What we need is a little deeper in." She took his niece by the hand and led them all toward a wall at the back of the section, to where what looked like sports bras hung. "You don't need anything fancy, and nothing needs to be poking you or prodding you."

Mia nodded, looking around. "Which one do I get?"

"Something like this." Lizzie plucked a plain white t-back sports bra off a display hook, and Max let out a breath he didn't realize he was holding. If Mia needed something with more structure and supportive cups and all that jazz he would absolutely buy it for her, but he couldn't help but be relieved to learn that for now, what she needed was simple. She was only nine; she had plenty more time in her life for complicated.

He didn't want to screw this up, and most of what he knew about female bodies and how to appreciate them was ... not applicable in this situation. He let his gaze flick over to Lizzie for a bare second, but he couldn't think about how much he appreciated her body or he'd embarrass himself in the bra section at Kohl's.

He was going to have to read up on healthy approaches to women's bodies, he realized abruptly.

He knew perfectly well the kinds of pressure women faced in society, and what it could do to them— Angelica had shared some very frank stories during their cooking lessons about the differences in her life between her modeling days and when she'd become a 'curvy' actress, and what it had done to her confidence —and she had some of the healthiest self-esteem he'd ever seen. He needed to learn more about how to help Mia with that sort of thing.

Lizzie reached up to pull three more options down off the wall. "Okay. Let's go try them on," she said, guiding Mia toward the dressing room.

He followed behind, discovering a leather bench that he sat on just outside the door while they proceeded inside. After Lizzie had come and gone twice more with different options, he realized they might be a while. He stood and moved closer to the entrance of the fitting room. "Hey," he called out to them. "I'm going to go, uh, look at some stuff for me."

"Okay, we'll be here," Lizzie called back from some- where in the depths of the long room.

He made his way back to the charm bracelet display Mia had been looking at, and picked one up. They were pretty cute, he had to admit as he bounced it gently in his palm. He picked up a bracelet that featured a unicorn charm, then hunted through the rest of the options and found two more that he liked: one was a paint palette, and the other a heart. He tucked them under his arm and turned to walk away, then turned back, a bracelet with a delicately forged anchor affixed to it catching his eye.

Before he could change his mind, he added it to his haul and carried it all over to the register. Lizzie might think it was just a cute nautical charm, but he'd know its significance—she was his anchor. She grounded him, and made his life calm in the heavy, turbulent seas of life. Mia adored her, too.

He'd give her the bracelet, and maybe when she sailed into the future she deserved, she'd let him add more charms for more memories they could make together.

Twenty minutes later he returned to find they were still at it. "I'm back," he called.

"Almost done," Lizzie said, and he heard what sounded like Mia giggling.

"Take your time." He sat back down on the bench and stretched his legs out.

"Max Vergaras?" The voice was familiar. "What are you doing here?" It was Sean's mother, Mary Amory. She ran The Breadery, and had for as long as Max had lived in River Hill. They'd worked together frequently —Frankie's made most of their own breads and desserts, but occasionally Max ordered something special from the bakery across the square. And they often catered the same community events. Sean had taken on a lot more of the bakery's day-to-day operations in the last year, which allowed his mom to take more time for herself these days.

"I'm, uh, waiting for Mia and—" He stopped as his niece and Lizzie came out of the fitting room.

Mary's gaze turned shrewdly assessing, and her eyes flicked between Max and Lizzie with more interest than he thought was warranted.

"Hi," Lizzie said, seemingly unfazed by the older woman's open perusal. "I'm Lizzie."

Max liked living in a small town most of the time, but once in a while it could be overwhelming—like when your friend's mother was trying to sniff out potential gossip. Lizzie, bless her, seemed to just roll with it, though.

"Mary Amory," Sean's mom said, her eyes bright as she turned to his niece. "And you must be Mia."

Mia nodded, her hand creeping into Lizzie's. "Hi."

"Amory? You must be Sean's mother," Lizzie remarked. "And I guess that makes you Jess's mother-in-law, too." She nudged Mia. "We love Jess." Mia nodded, still silent.

Mary Amory grinned. "I love Jess, too." She smiled down at Mia. "She's mentioned you quite a bit." Jess had done some of the babysitting before Angelica's mother had come to town and taken everything over with Big Grandma Energy.

Mia smiled shyly, but her previous outgoing attitude had disappeared. She still struggled with new people a bit, returning to her introverted ways when meeting strangers. Her therapist had assured Max it was nothing to worry about.

"So," Max said, trying to steer the conversation to its conclusion. While he'd been told not to worry about Mia's shyness, he didn't want to subject her to something that made her uncomfortable if he didn't have to. "Are you two finished?"

Mia and Lizzie nodded in unison.

"Well, I do love a nice family shopping trip. You all look so happy together." Mrs. Amory beamed at all three of them.

"Oh, we're not—"

"We don't—"

Max and Lizzie spoke at the same time, and then glanced at each other. A slight flush was rising on Lizzie's cheeks, and Max felt his own reddening.

Mary appeared oblivious. "It's been lovely running into you! Enjoy your day. I've got more shopping to do. In the baby section." She looked like she might explode with excitement at the thought of her impending grandchild, and Max hastened to get his not-quite-family away.

"Nice to see you," he called over his shoulder as he shepherded Lizzie and Mia out of the embarrassment zone.

He didn't realize he had his arm around Lizzie's waist until Mia pulled free of his other hand as they reached the line for the cash register, giving them a look that was alarmingly speculative and too much like Mary's had been a few seconds before. He yanked away, and Lizzie looked up at him, startled. Her cheeks turned a soft shade of pink. It was so easy to be comfortable together, and they slipped into a family unit so quickly. Max honestly wasn't all that sure he wanted to slip back out.

Maybe Mary Amory had been right after all.

16

izzie pulled into a parking space at St. Aloysius and checked her reflection in the rearview mirror to make sure that she was presentable. She hadn't planned on coming tonight, but when Mia had called her up yesterday afternoon and said it would mean a lot to her, how could she say no?

Ever since their trip to Kohl's a few weeks ago, she and Mia had been spending a lot of time together. First, Lizzie had driven her to the library to photocopy a handful of pages from an out-of-print book for a project she was working on for school. Then she'd taught her how to play chess for a different school project.

And now that Mia was displaying some of her artwork for her school's annual exhibit, she'd come along for this too, even though she'd been worried it might be awkward. The only reason Lizzie hadn't begged off was because Angelica had assured her everyone else was coming, too. Except here Lizzie was in the parking lot, and she didn't recognize a single car other than Max's. Unless they'd all suddenly taken up clowning, eight adults hadn't ridden with him.

Maybe she was early. Lizzie checked the clock on her dashboard to find that no, she was actually late. Muttering under her breath about the reliability of her new friends, she opened her car door and stepped out. Striding toward the low brick building with her head bent forward against the cold, she didn't see the hard wall of male muscle looming in front of her until she smacked into it and careened backward. In the time it took her to let out a startled *oof*, a pair of hands shot out to pull her upright.

"Thank you, I—" Her gaze shot up, and she locked eyes with Max.

"Lizzie?"

"Oh, hello. I, um, didn't see you there." Her voice sounded more breathy than usual, but it was easy to blame it on her surprise—not the fact that he was so handsome in his dark denim jeans and burgundy cashmere sweater, the deep, vibrant color setting off the amber in his irises so perfectly that she found it hard to breathe.

His lips quirked to the side. "So I gathered." He stood smiling down at her, his palms still locked around her biceps, as she looked up into eyes that flashed with good humor.

"Mia invited me," she blurted after several seconds of quiet stretched between them.

"Yeah, she said she was going to." His palms coasted slowly down the length of her arms, his eyes following their movement until he reached her fingers. He squeezed them gently, hooked their pinkies together ever so briefly, and then dragged his hands away. "I hope that was okay."

It was the most innocent of touches, but Lizzie felt it deep in her bones—and elsewhere. Had a simple caress ever been so tantalizing? She was thankful she'd decided to wear a turtleneck so he wouldn't see the goosebumps that had broken out along her arms.

"Of course. You know I adore Mia."

"I do know that."

Lizzie watched as the humor faded from his gaze and was replaced with a look of pure longing. She recognized the look; she frequently wore it herself. Sometimes, when she was feeling particularly weak, she wondered why they continued to fight this thing that existed between them. Sometimes, in the quiet of her heart, she thought her career might not be worth it. But then Lizzie would remember who she was and how hard she'd worked to achieve everything that she had, and she'd bolster her resolve all over again.

But standing outside Mia's school in the chilly February evening in front of Max, she found herself back in one of her weak moments.

"Should I go?" she whispered, pushing her hair behind her ears in an effort to keep her hands busy. Otherwise, she might be tempted to cup his cheek in her palm and rub her thumb over his stubble. He shaved every morning, she knew, but come evening, his jaw would be shadowed with the beginnings of what would be a thick, dark beard if he ever let it grow for more than a day. She'd seen traces of it the night she'd spent at his house, and ever since then she'd secretly wondered if it would be soft to the touch if he grew it out. She also wondered how it would feel between her thighs.

He shot a quick glance over his shoulder toward the school and then brought his gaze back around to her. "No, actually, but I'd avoid room 102 if I were you."

"Why? What's in there?"

He chuckled and shook his head in bemusement. "More than I wanted to see about religious instruction. Nuns, man. I think they forget these are just kids."

"Let me guess, lots of fire and brimstone?"

"One of the third graders made a diorama representing the Gates of Hell."

"No!"

He chuckled again. "Yes."

"Wow."

"Yeah, wow."

Their conversation tapered off, and while Lizzie knew she should move on, she stayed rooted to her spot.

So did Max.

Eventually, his smile faded. "How are you, Lizzie?" He moved to touch her, but then—almost as if he thought better of it—dropped his hand back down to his side where his fingertips beat a rhythm against his thigh.

She swallowed deeply. "I'm … okay." She'd been tempted to say she was good, but she'd never lied to Max before, and she didn't intend to start now. "Still trying to figure some things out, you know?"

He nodded slowly. "Yeah, I know."

"How are *you*?"

He rocked back on his heels and blew out a breath. "The truth?"

"Always."

"I miss you," he whispered. She opened her mouth to say something—anything—but before she could get the unknown words out, he continued. "I know why we can't be together, and I respect that. I just … well, I miss my friend. Noah's meme game is seriously lacking." He smiled then, but Lizzie noticed it didn't quite reach his eyes.

"If it makes you feel any better, Angelica's is pretty terrible, too."

His lips quirked. "Speaking of, are you going over there tomorrow night?"

"I don't know," she hedged, wondering what his plans were. Angelica had sent her an invitation to a dinner party yesterday, but … "It seems more like a couples thing, don't you think?"

"I'm kind of used to it by now, to be honest. With them all paired off, I'm the lone hold out." Max chuckled and scratched his chin.

"The lone holdout," she repeated slowly.

How long would that last though? Every day she woke up wondering if today was the day some beautiful, smart, cultured woman would walk into Frankie's and steal him away. Not that he was hers, of course, but she hated to think of him as anyone else's either. It was wildly unfair of her, but she couldn't seem to help herself.

"It's not so bad, I swear," he continued. "But if you were to come, I'd have a friend to keep me company when Iain and Naomi start sucking face across the table."

"So I'd be saving you then, is what you're saying?" She injected her voice with as much false humor as she could muster. She couldn't let him know just how badly she wanted to be the one sucking face. Although maybe not at the dinner table.

He nodded, his tongue flicking out to lick a path over his bottom lip, and wild horses couldn't have dragged Lizzie's gaze away. "Yes, exactly. So you'll come?"

Her mind was telling her to say no, but her heart was urging her to say yes. In the end, she went with her heart. "Yeah, I'll come."

THERE WAS COINCIDENCE, and then there was conspiracy, and Lizzie was beginning to think her repeated run-ins with a certain sexy chef were one big old conspiracy.

Not by him, mind you. Every time they ran into each other, he seemed just as surprised—if not more so—to see her. Not including last week's art show at Mia's school and subsequent dinner party, this was the sixth time this month she'd been invited somewhere only for Max to be leaving just as she arrived, or arriving just as she left, or the rest of the gang to be absent entirely. No doubt about it, his friends were working overtime to make sure they spent time together.

It would have been hilarious ... if it weren't happening to her. But since it was, it was just frustrating instead.

She might not be actively avoiding Max any longer, but that didn't mean she wasn't still worried about the state of her license. If only she could get clarification one way or the other, things would be so much easier.

As it was, she continued to try and find an answer to the questions plaguing her every waking moment while she waited to hear back from the positions she'd applied to.

Over the past couple of weeks, she'd spoken with a lawyer who specialized in family court, a therapist, and one of her former professors. The lawyer had glibly assured Lizzie there was no cause for concern if she were to pursue a romantic relationship with Max, but had also added that if anyone *did* try to revoke her license or sue her, the firm would be happy to take her case. She couldn't help but feel like their advice was more about what they could gain than her happiness and well-being.

The therapist had been even less help than the lawyer. What had started off as a fairly straight-forward conversation had ended with Lizzie being directed to talk about her feelings regarding her dead parents—a topic that had been analyzed ad nauseum when she was a teenager. While there was a lot about her relationship with Max that she didn't understand, she knew well enough that it had absolutely nothing to do with the similarities between herself and Mia.

And her former professor? Well, the woman might actually be senile now, because she'd sworn a lot more than Lizzie had remembered from her lectures. Plus, twice during their conversation, she'd gone off on a rant about how The Man was sticking it to Lizzie. Frankly, she hadn't been sure if Professor Wilkinson meant figuratively or literally, since she'd also made *boom chicka boom boom* sounds while thrusting her hips suggestively. It had been a deeply alarming experience.

Despite Lizzie's best efforts, she was no closer to finding a solution to her *can-I-or-can't-I?* problem than she'd been when this whole thing started, and she *still* didn't have a job. But since she couldn't find anything concrete telling her it was forbidden to simply be friends with Max either, she'd decided to stop fighting it. Which meant inviting him to sit next to her during the mid-day screening of the latest big budget heist movie was entirely on the up-and-up.

"Fancy meeting you here," she said, strolling up behind him in the concession line.

He glanced over his shoulder, and then turned around to face her, his mouth split into a friendly, happy smile. "Hey, you," he said, leaning down to envelop her in a tight hug.

She tried not to hyperventilate as his arms wrapped around her. "Hey," she said back when he stepped away and shoved his hands down into the front pockets of his jeans. "What are you doing here?"

"I've been dying to see this movie, but between Mia's schedule, the restaurant, and prepping for Noah and Angelica's wedding, I haven't had the time. Wendy finally kicked me out of the restaurant, threatening to reveal all the spoilers if I didn't just go already."

Lizzie laughed. She didn't know Wendy well, but she'd heard enough stories about Max's chef de cuisine to know the woman would absolutely make good on her threats.

"What about you?" he asked.

Lizzie hated to admit it to anyone, least of all Max, but the truth was, she was bored out of her mind sitting home alone in her house day after day, so when Maeve had asked her to join her, she'd jumped at the chance despite not having seen the two previous movies in the franchise. Unfortunately, Maeve canceled at the very last minute—something about stills and pressure valves at the distillery. But since Lizzie was already dressed and heading down the highway, she'd decided to go alone.

"I was supposed to meet Maeve here, but something came up so ..." she shrugged. Honestly, the way things were going, she wasn't all that surprised to see Max here instead of Maeve.

His mouth turned down into a frown. "Weird. Ben said yesterday he might join me, but then this morning he texted to say he was taking Maeve up to Mendocino instead." His brows deepened into a vee. "You don't think—"

Lizzie barely managed to contain her laughter as he came the same realization she'd had several days ago. "—that this was all a set up?"

"A set up," he stated flatly.

"Yes, exactly. I mean, how many times have we 'coincidentally' run into each other lately?" She held up her hands to make air quotes.

A rueful smile tugged his lips to the side. "I'd expect this from Angelica, but Ben and Iain are a surprise. Those bastards."

"It's not just your friends though," she pointed out. "I'm pretty sure Mia's in on it too."

"Mia? How?"

She tilted her head and gave him a *look*. "That girl calls me practically every day, and I finally figured out the other day it wasn't just to chat. She's been getting my schedule, and then, I believe, ferrying it to Naomi, who passes it along to Angelica. I'm convinced it's one big conspiracy to have us spend time together."

He chuckled. "They're good."

She nodded. "They are."

"You said you figured it all out the other day?"

"Honestly, I've had my suspicions for awhile."

"And yet you still came when Maeve invited you to see a movie," he said, his voice laced with something warm and a little bit cocky. Max wasn't an arrogant man by any means, but Lizzie couldn't lie—confidence looked *good* on him.

"And still I came," she agreed as her heart kicked wildly against her chest.

Eyes the color of her favorite bourbon roved her face. "Well, I'm glad you did."

"Yeah, me too," she whispered.

He rocked back on his heels. "It might be presumptuous, but what are you doing after the movie?"

"Maeve and I were supposed to get dinner, so ..."

She shrugged. When Maeve had canceled, Lizzie had assumed she'd just head home after the movie and heat up another in a long line of bland microwave meals.

"Or we could go grab dinner," he suggested, his voice suffused with hope.

Briefly, Lizzie wondered if Max knew he wore his heart on his sleeve. Part of her liked the idea that he *did* know, but didn't care. There was something supremely sexy about a man who was comfortable sharing his feelings.

"That sounds great," she said, as they made their way side-by-side into the darkened theater.

17

I love her. I love her. IloveherIloveherIloveher. The litany had been charging through Max's mind for weeks and it showed no sign of abating.

And apparently his friends knew it too. Once Lizzie had clued him in on what they'd been doing, he'd been torn between a sense of indignation at their meddling and one of sheer gratitude. He would never have been able to get her to all of the events and places they'd conveniently run into each other on his own, especially not when she'd been scrupulously avoiding him.

Thankfully, that seemed like a thing of the past.

Although Max still didn't know what her career plans were; over dinner the other night, she'd told him that she'd applied to several jobs and was just waiting to hear back. More surprisingly, she had also shyly confessed that she'd applied to graduate school, hoping to get into a program for children's play therapy. He'd listened to her explanation of the field and marveled—both at how she practically glowed from within while describing it, and how he'd instantly known it was perfect for her. Something he'd had no problem telling her. She'd flushed with pleasure and cautioned him not to get too excited; it had been a long time since she'd been in school.

"Yeah, but you have years of experience in a related field," he'd pointed out. "They'd be nuts not to accept you."

"From your lips to the admissions officer's ears," she'd said, and they'd moved on to other topics.

It had been a long time since Max had sat around talking until two o'clock in the morning, and he'd paid dearly for it the next day with a raging headache that no amount of coffee could penetrate, but he wouldn't have traded those long hours with her for anything in the world.

Now, he stared down at the invitation in his hand and decided it was time to make his move. Grad school or no grad school, he wanted Lizzie in his life. There had to be a way to make their relationship work. He couldn't believe the state would try to take away her license if she were in a different job than the one she'd met Mia in, and if they did try? Well. Last night he'd realized a fairly relevant fact: he had a damned good lawyer in his back pocket.

He picked up his phone and tapped out the message before he could think about it more.

Max: Hey, I have a question.

Lizzie: Go for it.

Max: Will you go to Noah and Angelica's wedding with me?

Lizzie: … awkward.

Max: It won't be, I promise!

Lizzie: No, I mean, I already have my own invitation.

Max: What?

She sent him a picture of her invitation sitting on her kitchen counter. It was addressed to Ms. Elizabeth Teague. He squinted. It also said 'and guest,' just like his did. Clearly, Angelica was trying to give him a heart attack.

Max: Rehearsal dinner, too? Are you taking a plus one?

Lizzie: Yes, rehearsal too. Not planning on a date, unless it's Mia.

Max: She got her own invitation.

Lizzie: Aw, that's so sweet of Angelica.

He agreed. Mia's squeal when she'd seen her name in embossed script on the elegant cream envelope had been worth every snarky comment Angelica had ever made to him.

Max: Well, if I can't convince you to come to the wedding as my date, can I convince you to come taste-test some final food options?

Lizzie: Shouldn't that be Angelica's job?

Max: I need to narrow things down a little more. I'd rather just give her two or three choices, but I have like fifteen different ideas.

Lizzie: So you're saying I should come hungry?

Max: Are you saying you're coming?

Lizzie: I'll bring my own fork.

Max: I think I can provide a fork. My place?

Lizzie: Not the restaurant?

Max: Wendy's wife sent me an email saying I wasn't allowed to do any more wedding stuff in the kitchen until crunch time because she hasn't budgeted for a vow renewal this year and Wendy's getting too many ideas.

When Lizzie sent him three laugh emojis followed quickly by a promise to meet him at his place tomorrow night, he rubbed his hands together, feeling extremely smug.

The next night, he laid out several dishes in front of her and handed her a sheet of paper.

She looked surprised. "You made all these just now?"

He grinned. "No, I cheated. I added a few of my

ideas to the Frankie's menu this week, so Wendy and the crew made them." He pointed. "That one, and that one, and the duck, over there. I did the appetizer choices here, but most of the entrees came home with me."

"Sneaky," she said, an admiring tone in her voice.

"It's almost like I do this for a living," he teased her.

Her cheeks pinked. "I didn't mean—"

"I know," he said quickly. "You're right, though, I don't usually do a ton of wedding catering. It's usually town events or party-style stuff where I'm bringing out the chafing dishes and my staff handles a lot of it."

She nodded. "I remember seeing Frankie's on a lot of advertising for events all over Sonoma. I never had time to go to any of them, though." She sobered. "I do now, I guess."

The last thing he wanted her thinking about tonight was her stalled career. "Something will come up," he said as breezily as he could manage. "In the meantime, you *do* have an important job. Open up that paper."

She unfolded the sheet he'd handed her and looked down, lips quirking to the side as she read through the chart he'd printed. "This is some pretty intense flavor profiling you're asking me to do."

"Um, it's Angelica Travis's wedding," he said. "Do I need to say more?"

She laughed. "I'm not sure I'm qualified to judge if something is—" she squinted. "Flavor-popping? What's this one? Divine intervention?"

He leveled her with an expression of mock sternness. "Try the food before you comment on my categories."

She dug into her purse, hung on the back of the chair she was sitting in, and emerged triumphantly holding a utensil. "I brought a fork."

"You're ridiculous," he said fondly, letting the swell of warmth that was washing through his body as he watched her at his kitchen table seep into his voice.

"Hey, it's an important job. You said so yourself." She surveyed the plates covering the table as he took a seat opposite her. "What's first?"

"This one." He grabbed his own fork and stuck it into the first appetizer. "Sweet potato beignet with avocado crema."

She stabbed one of the little balls of fried dough and popped it into her mouth. "Mmrph nng."

He was distracted by watching her lips move. "What?"

She swallowed. "This one for sure."

"It's the first one you've tried!"

She shrugged. "Better keep impressing me, I guess." The corner of her lips tilted up into a sly smile, and he nearly leapt over the table to kiss her.

In due time.

Instead, he fed her some more. And some more after that. They made their way through a plate of smoked pork belly with apple chutney, which was promptly added to her list of keepers, and egg yolk ravioli with an herb butter sauce, which didn't. "Jess is pregnant," she said. "No runny egg yolks."

"That's a thing?"

"Mm-hmm."

On to squash fritters —"Not as good as the beignets, sorry"—and cod Wellington with frizzled prosciutto. Lizzie stole his portion after she'd finished eating her own.

"So that's a yes, then?"

"Shhh," she said, chewing. "Leave me with my new best friend."

He laughed, and moved on to the entrees. He'd been watching his customers' reactions to them all week, but he wanted Lizzie's opinion even more. He wanted her opinion on everything, to be honest.

She liked the beef tenderloin, pronounced the braised short ribs to be better, thought the chicken was boring, and declared that she wanted to write poetry about the pasta in truffle and taleggio cream sauce.

"If Angelica doesn't pick this one, I'm going to throw her another wedding so she can make the right choices the next time," she said.

"You have some sauce on your cheek." Without thinking, Max reached across the table to remove it with his thumb. When his fingers brushed against her skin, they both froze.

After a moment when Max was sure she could hear his heart thundering in his chest, he swiped the sauce from her face and brought his thumb to his mouth.

Her eyes followed the movement, and he watched her pupils dilate as he slowly sucked the sauce from his finger. He swallowed harder than was strictly necessary for three drops of cheese sauce. "Lizzie…"

"Yes," she breathed.

"Can we——-"

"—Yes," she answered, not bothering to hear the rest of his question before shoving her chair back. She stood, and held her hand out to him.

He wrapped his fingers around hers and let her tug him upright, the motion carrying their bodies closer. His hands curved around her waist and his fingers dipped into the waistband of the form-fitting cotton pants that molded perfectly to the curves of her hips. An old heather-gray tee that was so thin from years of wear that parts of it were see-through completed her outfit. She'd told him with a laugh that they were her eating clothes, indicating the elastic waistband, but he could think of a lot of other uses for them. Preferably ones that involved him taking them off of her.

"Do you know," he said, gritting the words out low and gravelly, "how hard it has been not to undress you every time I've seen you over the last month?"

Her hands were busy at his waist. "Probably about as hard as this." Her fingers dove into his jeans, curving around his cock inside his boxers, and his hips thrust against the pressure helplessly.

He groaned. "Lizzie." He needed her naked. Immediately.

"Bedroom?" she gasped.

Giving fervent mental thanks to the new friend who had invited Mia over for a sleepover tonight, he maneuvered them out of the kitchen. They made it as far as the couch.

She hooked her leg around his knee and sent him tumbling with a push to his shoulders.

"Where'd you learn that move?" he protested as his back hit the cushions.

"Shhh," she said. "A magician never reveals her secrets." Then she did something else that made his shirt fly off his chest. "Voila!"

God, he loved her. He opened his mouth to tell her, and then paused. Was she ready to hear it? Was he definitely ready to say it? There was so much that was still so uncertain in both of their lives. For starters, he'd signed a contract last week committing himself to opening another restaurant down in Silicon Valley, two hours away from River Hill. At the time, he'd thought it would be a good distraction, not to mention it'd expand his name recognition well beyond the confines of wine country.

Now, with Lizzie in his arms pulling her own shirt up over her head, he wondered if he was just avoiding the hard truth about their future together. She still hadn't heard about any of the jobs she'd applied to, or graduate school. But when she did—

"If you're thinking about Angelica's wedding right now, I will actually murder you," she said pleasantly.

"I'm thinking about you." He reached for her. The best way to stop thinking was to act, after all.

His hands skimmed over her sides as he drew her down to him, her body covering his in a way that made every nerve thrum with pleasure. He kissed her, and she slid her tongue along the seam of his lips. They opened to each other, and she made a sound that went straight to his groin as he drove his fingers into her hair to cup the back of her head.

Writhing and twisting against each other, they somehow managed to remove their pants and underwear without him being aware of actually doing it. Skin to skin, suddenly, everything was faster, harder, hotter. She handed him a condom—where had that come from? She really was a magician—and he tore it open and rolled it on as she slid her cool fingers around his balls, making him moan. Then she rose up over him, hair falling down around her shoulders like a goddess, and slid herself up, over, and down. She paused, thighs trembling, with the tip of his cock barely inside her. He looked up at her to find her staring down at him with a whole world in her eyes. And when she sank down, taking him deep inside her, he kept his eyes open, letting her see what he couldn't say.

He loved her. He wanted her. He didn't know what their future might hold, but he'd fight for them as long as he could.

18

izzie lifted her glass to toast to Angelica and Noah's happiness. For the past hour, she'd listened as those gathered at Frankie's to celebrate the couple's upcoming nuptials told both hilarious and touching stories about how the two had found love.

Lizzie had heard Angelica's condensed version of the story at book club, of course, and Max had once told her that Noah had done a complete one-eighty once he realized he needed to soften his hard edges if he was going to convince Angelica to give him a chance, but it was heartwarming nonetheless to hear these small anecdotes from others. As the toasts and stories continued, Noah ate it up. She'd never seen him more confident, or more in his element.

Every so often, Lizzie had wondered how his and Angelica's relationship worked. While he'd been nothing but kind to her, she knew how to read people —see the things they wouldn't say aloud—and she'd sensed that underneath his indulgent smiles and good-natured joking was a man who had fought hard to get to a place where those things came easy to him. Once, she'd spied him taking a phone call as he was on his way out of the inn just as she was coming in, and he'd been wearing a scowl so fierce it had nearly stopped her in her tracks. By way of apology, Angelica had said, "Don't mind him. He's not always this grumpy, he's just had a bad day."

On the flip side, she wasn't sure Angelica had *ever* had a bad day. Or if she had, she'd turned it into something better by sheer force of will. Lizzie had never met someone who was so fundamentally positive about everything without being remotely obnoxious about it. If a situation was less than ideal, Angelica would acknowledge it, determine how best to deal with it, and then move on. Frankly, the woman was a force of nature.

Now that she thought about it, maybe *that* was what made Angelica and Noah's relationship work. Perhaps opposites really did attract, and the two were stronger as a unit than as individuals. It was a cliche as old as time, and yet, there was no denying that Noah and Angelica were two of the most solidly in love people Lizzie had ever met.

Maybe there's something in the water here, she thought as her gaze drifted fondly over her friends. They were *all* like that.

Intentionally childfree and committed to never getting married, Iain and Naomi had the most unconventional relationship of the group, whereas Sean and Jess were the most traditional, especially now that they were gearing up to expand their little family. And yet, she wouldn't say one couple was more in love than the other. Their love was just ... different.

And then there were Maeve and Ben, a couple that was so sweet and caring toward one another, while somehow managing to also be so utterly *hot* that more than once Lizzie'd had to excuse herself when all they'd been doing was *looking* at each other.

Briefly, she wondered what people would say about her and Max. The man was patience and sweetness personified—look at how he'd welcomed Mia into his life, or how he'd spent his entire career feeding people just to see them happy. But he was also damned sexy. And all that goodness, and sweetness, and just sheer wonderfulness didn't mean he wasn't good in bed. In fact, she'd argue that was what made him the best damn lover she'd ever had. Just thinking about their time together last weekend had her toes curling in her heels.

"Penny for your thoughts?"

Lizzie jumped, bringing her palm flat against her chest. "Oh my god, Maeve. You scared me."

The Irish woman peered at her curiously. "I can see that."

"I was just thinking ..."

"—About how ridiculously happy Noah looks today?"

Lizzie nodded, relief washing through her. From the way Maeve was watching her, she'd been worried she was about to be grilled about the specifics of *those* thoughts. "He can't stop smiling."

Maeve chuckled. "I should think not. He's been trying to get Angelica to marry him for a long time. It wasn't until Jess and Sean came home from Costa Rica with a ring on her finger that she finally relented."

"Well, Angelica does love jewelry," Lizzie chuckled.

"That she does," Maeve said. "What about you?"

Lizzie swung her gaze from the soon-to-be-married couple to the younger woman at her side. "What about me?" she asked cautiously.

"You don't wear much jewelry," Maeve pointed out, doing a visual once-over of Lizzie. Aside from a pair of tiny diamond studs she'd worn every day since her uncles gave them to her on her eighteenth birthday, she was unadorned.

"Noooo ... but then, you don't either," Lizzie deflected. She didn't know where this conversation was heading, but she was distinctly uncomfortable with the increasingly assessing look on the other woman's face.

Maeve fingered the delicate gold chain at her wrist, her eyes briefly darting across the room to where Ben and Max were chatting near the bar. "I can't wear jewelry at work, of course. As for when I'm off, well, I might not have been a fan of it in the past ... but you never know."

From Maeve's tone, Lizzie got the distinct impression they weren't talking about just any old piece of jewelry anymore. Maybe it was the two glasses of champagne she'd had, or maybe it was the setting and overall mood of the rehearsal dinner, but Lizzie found her tongue loosening. "What about Ben? How does he feel about, um, jewelry?"

Slowly, Maeve brought her gaze back around, her smile sly and knowing. "Why do you ask?"

"Well," Lizzie said, nervously shifting her weight onto her other foot. She didn't want to pry, but if she was reading the undertones of their conversation correctly, marriage was the next logical step for the couple. Not that she was one to talk about what was logical when it came to relationships. After all, she'd let herself fall for a man she knew was off limits. "I just mean, um, do you think you'll ever ..." She twirled her finger in the air as if to indicate all the pomp and circumstance of the pre-wedding celebration.

Maeve lifted her shoulders in a light shrug. "You never do know." Her eyes landed on something over

Lizzie's shoulder, and her easy smile morphed into one that belied much deeper feelings. "I hate to be rude," she said, setting a hand on Lizzie's arm, "but if you'll excuse me ..."

She was gone before Lizzie could even say goodbye.

With an empty glass and no one else around who she knew well enough to talk to, Lizzie used Maeve's departure as an excuse to visit the ladies' room. Frankly, their conversation had unnerved her. If she were being honest with herself, practically everything about this night had been unnerving.

While she and Max had exchanged warm hellos upon her arrival, they'd barely spoken ten words since. Not that she'd expected anything more than that. When she'd left his house the other day, things had still been so uncertain between them. With so much of her life currently up in the air, she'd been unable to commit to him the way she knew he wanted her to.

But as with everything else about their relationship, he'd been so *good* about it. So understanding. "Take all the time you need," he'd said with a lingering kiss to her forehead as he ushered her to her car before Mia returned home from her sleepover.

With her body sated and her heart full, she'd wanted to tell him that she didn't need any more time. That she was all in. But somehow she couldn't bring herself to say the words.

Since applying for the job in Miami and not getting it, she'd also applied for lesser positions in Boston and

Charlotte. They weren't what she wanted, but Lizzie could only hold out for so long as her savings were slowly dwindling away. And she'd all but given up hope on getting accepted to the grad school she'd applied to. It was the opportunity she was still most excited about, but the date for acceptance notification had passed last week with not so much as a peep. Some people might think no news was good news, but in this case, she couldn't help but feel like she'd been passed over.

With one last lingering glance toward where Max was standing talking to Angelica's mom, Lizzie wondered if not getting the job in Miami and not being accepted to the program were the signs she'd been waiting for. Maybe the universe was telling her that giving up her career to be with Max and Mia was the right move. There were worse things in life than a loving boyfriend.

And yet, she couldn't bring herself to believe that. She'd worked too hard and for too long to get to where she was to just, what ... give up? No, she couldn't reconcile that. And yet it seemed like the only way she could be with him was to do just that.

Whoever said women really could have it all can go jump in a lake, Lizzie thought. Because as far as she could tell, she could either have her career, or she could have Max. Both were simply not an option. She would have found a way by now if it were.

With a heavy heart, she stepped into a bathroom

stall and sank down onto the closed toilet seat. Heedless of the makeup she'd spent nearly an hour applying, she let her face fall into her open palms. For the next few minutes, she allowed herself to just *wallow*. She'd been holding back tears of frustration for days, and here, surrounded by so much love and happiness and hope for the future, she just couldn't take it anymore.

She was jobless. She was loveless. She was aimless. She was *tired*.

With that reality acknowledged, she wiped her nose, dabbed her eyes, and righted her appearance as best she could in the privacy of the small stall. Just then, she heard the sound of the bathroom door opening, and Naomi and Maeve's laughter floated toward her.

"Poor guy," Naomi said. "He's got it bad."

Maeve chuckled, but the loud noise from the hand dryer drowned out whatever she'd said in response.

Lizzie could have joined her friends then, but she didn't want them to know that she'd been crying. She'd have to explain *why*, and that would set off her tears all over again. So instead, she sat back down and pulled her feet up onto the toilet seat to wait them out. Just when she thought they were finally finishing up, the door to the bathroom opened *again*, and another set of women joined them. Lizzie didn't recognize the voices, but the women obviously knew Naomi as they immediately launched into what felt like might be a lengthy conversation about her upcoming exhibition.

Not wanting to eavesdrop, Lizzie reached into her purse and, as quietly as she could, slid her phone out, setting her thumb to the circle at the bottom to bring it to life. She refreshed her email app, and nearly jumped off her perch. With shaking hands, she clicked on the sender's name and clamped her emotions down in a stranglehold.

Dear Ms. Teague, we are writing to follow up on your acceptance to the graduate program in Counseling and Therapeutic Play at Patterson University. We sent you a letter of acceptance and an information packet to the address listed on your application, but as we have not heard back from you, I wanted to personally follow up to make sure that you are still interested in joining us for the Summer semester. If you could let me know your decision by March 21, we'd greatly appreciate it.

There was more, but Lizzie stopped reading.

She'd been accepted.

She let out the breath she'd been holding since seeing the program chair's name on her screen, and looked to the ceiling, tears forming anew.

She'd done it.

Despite not having taken the GRE; despite inching dangerously close to the backside of her thirties; despite not having a letter of recommendation from her last boss, she'd gotten into grad school. She was going to Portland!

Her elation quickly faded.

With a painful churning in her gut, she realized that also meant she was leaving Max and Mia. From somewhere deep inside her subconscious came a thought she'd never wanted to give voice to: *this was always going to happen.* All these weeks, she'd let herself outwardly believe that she might discover some hidden, magical way for them to be together, but that was never how their story was going to unfold.

Only now could she acknowledge that she'd known this all along.

It was why she'd put up one roadblock after another. Why even when she'd found professional articles to support pursuing a relationship with Max, she'd kept on looking for others that said the opposite. Consciously, she'd assumed she was trying her best to be with him. Subconsciously, however, she recognized that she'd actually been sabotaging any chance they'd ever had.

Because she was always going to leave him.

Whether for grad school or for one of those far-flung job opportunities, she'd been on her way out all along.

And now she wondered if by keeping him at arms' length, she'd been protecting them both.

She let out another long sigh, and realized the restroom had fallen quiet again. She listened for a few more seconds to make sure it wasn't just a lull in the conversation, and when she was confident she was alone, she slid from the stall. She checked her reflection in the mirror to make sure her makeup wasn't too badly smudged, and finding that it didn't look as bad as she feared, made her way to the door. She squared her shoulders, took a deep breath, and prepared herself to go back out there and wish the happy couple congratulations one final time before their wedding tomorrow.

I can do this.

That was her mantra the entire way down the hall and out into the main dining space. She kept repeating it to herself as she located Angelica and Noah off in the far corner, surrounded by a bevy of well wishers. Those were the words echoing in her head so loudly that she didn't hear her name being called until it was too late.

"Hey," Max said, stepping in front of her, effectively blocking her path. "I've been looking all over for you."

As quickly as she could, Lizzie pasted a mask of polite interest on her face. She couldn't let him see what she was really feeling. He didn't deserve to know what she'd only just discovered herself a few minutes ago.

She was in love with him, and she was going to leave him.

It was better if she only broke one of their hearts today.

"I'm sorry," she said, proud to hear her voice didn't shake the way her knees were. Quickly, she offered up a silent thanks for all the years of practice she had at masking her outward emotions while inwardly she wanted nothing more than to rail at the fates for all the ways the world was fucked up beyond belief. Not that she would ever equate her situation with some of the tragedies she'd witnessed over the years as a social worker, but if she could keep calm in the face of all of *that*, she could do so now—no matter what it might personally cost her. "I was in the bathroom. You know how it is. Lots of waiting in line."

Max peered down at her, his eyes flicking between hers with a touch of concern.

Her voice might not be shaking, but it *had* sounded overly bright, even to her own ears. She cleared her throat, and spoke again, hoping she could get out of there before her mask started to crack any further. "I was just going to say goodbye to Angelica and Noah, and then head home. I imagine you'll be here a bit longer though? "

He cleared his throat, too, and took a small, hesitant step forward. He lifted his right hand as if he was going to touch her, but then dropped it back down to his thigh where his fingers beat a staccato rhythm against his leg. "Another couple of hours, at least. Mr. and Mrs. Travis took Mia home with them since she was getting tired. I was hoping we could talk about—"

"Max?"

"Yeah?"

"Please, don't say it."

"Say what?" he asked. This time, when he lifted his

hand, he did reach out to take hold of Lizzie's. "What's wrong, baby?"

When Lizzie felt her bottom lip tremble at the quiet endearment, she bit down on it. Hard. She shook her head. "Nothing. Nothing's wrong."

He stared at her for a few beats in which she silently prayed for him to exercise a little bit of self preservation. But that wasn't who Max was, she knew. With him, everyone else always came first. "Lizzie … please. I love—"

She yanked her hand away and slapped her palm over his mouth. "I'm begging you. Please don't say it."

She watched as a bevy of emotions flashed across his expressive eyes. Confusion. Hurt. Anger. And then finally, resignation. Slowly, when she trusted him not to say the words that would break her, she dragged her hand away. "I just found out that I was accepted to grad school." His lips parted to speak, but she plunged on to prevent him from saying anything. "The program's at Patterson University. In Portland." It was at this point she realized that she'd never mentioned the program's location when they'd talked about it. Had she been vague on purpose? Had she lied by omission? Briefly, she wondered what else she'd kept locked inside of her instead of sharing with him.

Max took a tiny step back and shoved his hands deep into his pockets. "Congratulations," he said, he voice hoarse with heavy emotion. "I'm proud of you, Lizzie."

She wrapped her arms around her middle. "I have to take it, Max."

He nodded slowly as understanding settled over his handsome features. "Ah."

"Yeah. Ah."

"When do you leave?"

"I don't know exactly. Soon. The semester starts June first."

He nodded again. "Okay."

"Okay?"

He rocked back on his heels, and when he spoke next, his voice was more resolute. "Yes, okay. We'll figure this out."

She was about to tell him she didn't know how when they were interrupted. "There's an issue in the kitchen, boss. Wendy needs you ASAP."

Max cursed, and his head fell back to glare up at the ceiling. He muttered something that sounded suspiciously like *if the building isn't on fire I'm going to strangle her* as he pinched his nose and blew out a breath. After a few seconds, his face dropped forward again, and he stared beseechingly at Lizzie. "Stay. Please."

Lizzie held her breath for what felt like an eternity, but was probably only a second or two. Wendy wouldn't have sent someone looking for Max if it weren't truly important. Whatever was going on in the kitchen required his undivided attention, and he wouldn't be able to give it if she was sitting out here waiting for him to finish up. And yet, she also knew he wouldn't go investigate if she didn't agree to stay.

She crossed the fingers that were tucked up against her side and nodded.

Relief shone starkly in his amber eyes as he squeezed her arm. "Thank you."

When he turned to follow his young employee to the kitchen, Lizzie held her breath again. And the second he crossed through the swinging double doors, she let it out. She couldn't stop the tears that followed as she turned and practically ran for the door.

The building hadn't quite been on fire, but the grinding noises the main refrigerator had been making had been almost as bad. Between scrambling with his staff to find alternate storage for nearly all of the perishables for the wedding reception the next day, and then working with Wendy and one of the waiters who was getting a degree in mechanical engineering to haul the thing away from the wall, Max hadn't left the kitchen again until well past four o'clock in the morning.

By then, Lizzie had been long gone, and he couldn't blame her—he'd sent somebody to give her a message when he'd realized how bad the fridge situation was, but they hadn't been able to locate her in the chaos. He didn't know when, exactly, she left, but he had a sneaking suspicion that she'd snuck out shortly after he'd been abruptly called away. He knew her well enough to understand the look on her face as he'd turned to leave. He thought he had a pretty good idea of what had been going through her mind, and none of it was good.

He blew out a frustrated breath and scrubbed his hand over his face. He'd managed to get about an hour of sleep before it was time to be up again. He'd shaved as carefully as he could manage, thrown his tux in the Land Rover, and greeted a sleepy Ben, who'd agreed to take Mia over to The Oakwell Inn later. Leaving Ben to crash on his couch for another couple of hours until Mia woke up, Max had driven to Frankie's, distracting himself with prep work and cooking. Despite catering the wedding, the restaurant would stay open for both its regular lunch and dinner service, so he and Wendy had split up the tasks for today.

Now, he was done and ready to pack everything up. His catering manager, Piper, had just shown up with the van to transport the first load. Normally, when Max catered events, he spent his time behind the food, smiling and serving the guests. This was the first time he had to abandon his post to be a groomsman, but he trusted his staff implicitly. Piper, one of the most stoically calm people Max had ever met, had everything under control. It was only his nerves that made him triple-check everything.

All right. So maybe it wasn't just his nerves about the wedding acting up. This gnawing feeling in the pit of his stomach had nothing to do with catering or food. He could do all that in his sleep.

The reality was that he needed to talk to Lizzie, and until he did, he would continue to feel unsettled.

Unfortunately, when he arrived at The Oakwell Inn a few minutes later, she wasn't there. But that made sense, he told himself. She was only a guest, after all, not a member of the wedding party like himself. The bridesmaids—Naomi, Jess, and Maeve, and the Gentleman of Honor, Angelica's agent Jai, were fluttering around the house getting ready and bringing various things up to the largest of the guest suites, which Angelica had designated as the bridal suite. Noah, Sean, and Iain were over at the house next door, and Ben would join them after he dropped Mia off with Elaine Travis in an hour or so. Max would do the same after he helped Piper and the crew unload the van.

He checked his watch to note the time. Between now and when the wedding started, he didn't think he'd have a spare minute to track Lizzie down, but he'd have to try.

Three hours later, with a growing sense of urgency, he scanned the crowd seated in the inn's expansive back field. He stood next to Sean under a wide oak canopy that shaded them all from the sun's glowing rays. The baker stood next to Noah, as he'd refused to designate any of them as his best man. Because everyone knew Sean was the most responsible one among them, he'd been given the place of honor next to the groom to catch him if he fainted. There'd been a round of cheerful insults from Noah when they'd informed him of this plan, but he did look awfully pale as he waited for Angelica to come around the corner and make her entrance. He'd waited a long time for his bride. They all knew she was going to show up—she'd orchestrated what felt like the wedding of the century, after all—but the groom couldn't be blamed for a flicker of nervousness anyway.

Noah wasn't the only man standing up here who was fighting not to let his nerves get the best of him. Max surveyed the crowd again. He couldn't find Lizzie —hadn't seen her the entire time guests had been arriving, actually—and it was making him want to bolt for the end of the aisle to go and find her.

He'd known Angelica had invited a lot of people, but he hadn't quite realized what she'd meant when she'd smugly told him the wedding was going to be An Event, with capital letters so obvious you could hear them in her voice.

Half of River Hill was here, of course—Angelica was on the tourism board, and she knew every small business owner in town. Noah's family were celebrity winemakers in their own right, so Carter Bradstone was holding court with his socialite wife and daughters on the groom's side next to—Max squinted—was that the Clooneys? Sometimes he forgot that while Angelica was the celebrity—as evidenced by the flock of actresses crying prettily on the other side of the crowd—Noah had grown up in rarefied circles himself, though he usually pretended otherwise. Naomi's parents were here, too, which only made sense since she and Noah had known each other their whole lives, and their parents had once plotted to marry them off to one another.

In addition to it being his good friends' special day, Max knew he should be focusing on the fact that this was an opportunity for him. Everyone here was a potential client, some of them were potential investors, and Angelica had been blunt when she'd told him to impress them. "I heard about the franchising," she'd casually mentioned when she'd chosen the last few dishes for the menu. "Blow these people's minds, Max, and then sit back and watch as they throw their money at you."

Far be it from him to disobey a direct order from the star of RenoTV's flagship show. There were several network executives, as well as a few other renovation show hosts in the crowd, too. He let his eyes wander slowly over the guests one more time, recognizing a few of the local farmers on Noah's side, and a few actors on Angelica's side, before landing on the very last row.

There she was.

Lizzie sat quietly in the second chair in the row, penned in by Mia next to her, watching with a wistful expression on her face as Noah and Angelica said their vows. Max felt his entire body clench with the effort it took to not walk straight over to her.

Ben's knee nudged into his. "You all right?" Max gave a tiny nod, his eyes never leaving Lizzie.

After what felt like an eternity, Noah and Angelica wrapped up their vows. The mayor of River Hill, who'd cheerfully agreed to officiate when Angelica had asked, pronounced them married, and the bride wrapped her arms around the groom's neck to deliver a kiss that had the audience cheering. She ended it with a wink to someone who was wearing a press badge that indicated they were a photographer from *Martha Stewart Weddings*, and took Noah's arm for the processional down the aisle and back toward the inn.

Max followed them when it was his turn, his mind racing. He hoped Lizzie wouldn't vanish again. His time with her was coming to a close, and he knew deep in the marrow of his bones that if he didn't think of something, and soon, she'd hop on a plane to Portland and start her new life, the one he wanted to share with her, without ever knowing how he truly felt.

After a few frantic moments of weighing all of his options, Max did the only sensible thing he could think of. There was a time and a place for a grand gesture, and a wedding recessional wasn't it. He knew better than to do something outlandish that would turn him into a cautionary tale shared all over the internet, but he could get a message to one person subtly.

When he drew even with Lizzie and Mia, seated alongside the aisle at the end of their row, he gave Lizzie a warm smile and then bent to speak quietly and quickly into Mia's ear. "Whatever you do, don't let her leave."

Mia beamed at him and nodded as he passed. He kept going, never breaking his stride in the slow march back down the long lantern-dotted aisle. Once inside, he congratulated Noah, gave Angelica the required hug, and then left them to go check on his staff.

The reception was well underway by the time he managed to pull himself away from handling various minor emergencies. When he wasn't putting out small fires—both literally and figuratively—he'd been stopped multiple times by people who wanted to meet him and talk about restaurants. On any other day, at any other occasion, he would have been basking in it, smugly shaking hands and accepting business cards and outlining expansion plans with airy confidence. Today, all he wanted was to go find Lizzie before she left.

An hour later, he finally got his wish. She was sitting alongside Mia in the parlor, an oasis of quiet in the crowded inn as they chatted comfortably to each other. He sank down next to his niece, who immediately popped up onto her feet. "Took you long enough," she whispered loudly, any pretence of subtlety vanishing in the blink of an eye.

"Sorry." Max opened his mouth to explain himself, but she was already turning to leave, saying something about finding Mrs. Travis.

"I was starting to suspect something was up," Lizzie said.

He glanced over, and caught a look of amusement in her eyes. "Oh?"

"Mia's not really a chatterbox most of the time, so she was kind of stretching for material. Did you know baleen whales have two blowholes?"

He reached for her hand, and she let him take it. "Lizzie. I—"

"Don't ask me to stay, Max." She met his eyes, and the raw pain he saw there made his breath catch harshly in his lungs.

"I would never do that," he blurted. "You earned that spot, and you're going to be an amazing therapist."

She lowered her eyes, watching their fingers twine together. "Thank you."

"I just wanted to tell you how I feel," he said quietly. "And see if you felt the same."

"You know I do," she said.

He swallowed thickly. He'd thought so, but having her say it warmed every inch of him. "I love you, Lizzie."

"I love you too, Max. But I have to take this opportunity."

"I know. I want you to. I want you to have anything you want." He slid his thumb along her palm and cleared his throat. "What *do* you want, Lizzie?"

She met his eyes again, and there was something fierce in her gaze. "I want *everything*, Max. I want grad school, I want a job, and I want *you*."

"You can have me," he said.

"But I'm leaving."

He pressed his lips together around the smile that wanted to steal over his face. Lizzie was so used to denying herself to help others. But it was his turn to help her. "Lizzie. We're both adults, with careers that are important to us. I just signed a franchising deal to open another restaurant, and I have meetings set up for at least two more. I wasn't planning to live in your pocket. We can make long distance work while you're in school."

She stared at him. "Long distance?"

"People do it, you know. Think of it like this: you're going to be in Portland for two years, right? Assuming the program goes well, which it will, of course." She gave him a brief smile to reward his confidence in her, and he plunged on. "Opening another restaurant, maybe a few more—it's a lot of travel. And when I'm not traveling, there's Mia to focus on, too. But I want to call you every night, hear what you did that day, stay on the phone with you for an hour just to hear your voice. I want to visit you, and have you visit me, whenever we can."

He thought about one of the emails in his inbox that he hadn't answered yet, from an investment group in Portland. He'd once considered opening a restaurant in Oregon's hipster foodie mecca, but the idea of shuttling back and forth so often hadn't been all that appealing. Now, though, the idea had a lot more going for it. He wouldn't mention it to her just yet, though. Not unless the financing seemed viable and he could be assured he had complete control over the endeavor. Weekend visits would do for now.

"You think it would work?" she asked him with wide eyes. He watched her as realization, wonder, and finally hope flickered over her face.

"I *know* it would."

"But how? It's not like I'm moving down to San Jose. Portland's in a *whole other state*."

He suppressed a smile. "There are these magical things called planes, Lizzie. They carry people to and from destinations far and wide."

She swatted him on the shoulder. "I know what planes are, Max. I also know how expensive they can be."

"Maybe we each drive then, meeting halfway between here and there." He shrugged. "I don't have the exact answer right now, but I know there is one. We'll just have to get creative."

This time he didn't bother suppressing his smile.

Honestly, he was so damn giddy he wasn't sure that he could have. Saying these words out loud to her made his chest practically explode with the sheer amount of happiness he carried inside of him right now. "I love you, and I want to be with you. Whatever it takes to get you your dream job, I'm here for it. And when you graduate with honors, or flying colors, or whatever it is they give therapists, I'm here for that, too." He grasped her other hand so that he was holding both of them in his. "Please, Lizzie."

"Yes," she whispered slowly, as if she couldn't quite believe it. Then, more confidently, "Yes. Absolutely!"

He laughed, and tugged her forward into his arms. And finally, *finally*, he kissed her.

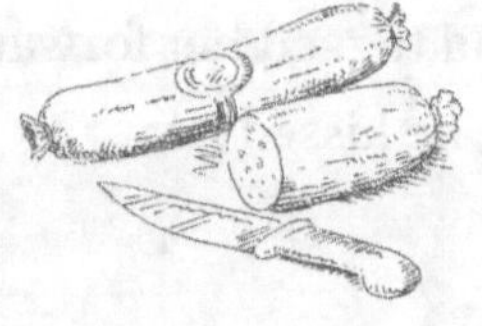

**** *Two Years Later* ****

*L*izzie stood at her kitchen table, her gaze bouncing between three distinct piles of papers. The first one was junk mail that needed to be recycled. The second pile was a copy of her lease and a note from her landlord asking her to sign it and return it by no later than next week if she wanted to keep living there. And finally, the third pile contained four flyers for open houses a friend who worked in real estate had given her this morning at yoga.

It had been a little over two years since she'd moved to Portland for grad school, and now that she'd graduated a couple of weeks ago, she had some decisions to make. Well, she and Max and Mia did, at any rate.

When he'd asked her to give a long distance relationship a shot, she hadn't known what to expect, but being separated by six-hundred-plus miles hadn't been as difficult as she'd feared. In fact, it had been surprisingly easy—once she'd gotten the hang of phone sex. Naomi had been more than willing to talk through the basics with her.

Not that she ever had to go too long between seeing him. The direct flight between Santa Rosa and Portland was less than two hours long—there were days he could reach her faster than if they'd driven down to San Francisco from River Hill during rush hour traffic. While at first she'd felt bad about him leaving Mia so often, they'd eventually worked out a system. On the weekends that he came up to Portland, his niece stayed with either Angelica's mom, or with Jess and Sean. She loved helping babysit their little girl almost as much as she loved painting.

And last summer, once Mia's school year had wrapped up, uncle and niece had spent the entire summer up in Portland so Max could open up a third outpost of Frankie's while Mia attended some special art camp Naomi had recommended. Lizzie's small apartment had been *very* cramped during their stay, but she'd adored having both of them around while she worked on her thesis project at a first-of-its-kind play therapy center.

It was during that stay that Max had first floated the idea of her getting a bigger place when her lease was up. The lack of space was the most obvious issue, but he also wanted to be closer to where he'd opened the restaurant when he came up. Not that Lizzie was opposed to moving across town; where she lived now was convenient to school, but not much else.

But for all he'd encouraged her to explore the neighborhoods of Southeast Portland, he'd been some-what vague about whether this potentially new place was hers, or theirs. Lizzie had absolutely zero reason to doubt Max's love for her, or his commitment to their relationship, but if she was going to pull up stakes and move, she wanted to know exactly what she was signing up for.

He was visiting, sans Mia, in a couple of days; they could discuss it all then. After she welcomed him back to town properly, of course. She was busy imagining all the ways that could play out—should she meet him at the door wearing nothing but a trench coat and high heels? Or perhaps she'd make him wait all day and night before they fell into bed together. There was a lot to be said for anticipation.

Except their relationship was nothing *but* anticipa-tion, and she didn't know if she'd be able to be near Max without wanting to undress him. So clearly it was sex first; conversation second. She was on her way to the coat closet in her small foyer when her phone rang. Pulling it out of her back pocket, she checked the screen to see that it was her former colleague Maggie calling.

They'd kept in touch after Lizzie had quit her job, but the majority of their interactions were done via Facebook or Instagram. While they'd emailed a couple of times over the last two years, and had gotten together for drinks when Lizzie had traveled to California last Thanksgiving, they weren't all *that* close. A phone call out of the blue was rather unexpected.

"Maggie?"

"You graduated, right?"

Lizzie's head jerked back and she held the phone away from her face to stare at it for a moment. That was a rather strange greeting, even for a woman as forthright as Maggie Beringer. She brought the device back to her ear and said, "Hello to you, too."

"Sorry about that," Maggie chuckled. "Hello, Lizzie. How are you?"

"Good. You?"

"Excellent! Fantastic! Which is why I'm calling."

"I did wonder."

"Please tell me you're still accredited in California, and that you have your counseling degree."

"Yes, on both accounts."

"Oh, thank god," Maggie breathed into her phone. "I was worried there for a minute."

Worried? "Why?"

"You remember that I took over Kate's job last year, right?"

Lizzie *did* remember. It was why she and Maggie had gone out for drinks, even though she'd only been in town for three days and hadn't wanted to leave the cozy confines of Max's house. But slaying the dragon that had been their boss was definite cause for celebration. "Congratulations, again."

"You're going to be doing more than congratulating me in a minute," Maggie said, her voice rising with excitement. "Do you also remember Roberta Jimenez?"

Lizzie scanned her brain to try and pull the name out of her memory. It sounded vaguely familiar, and yet ... "Oh! Yes. She ran that wellness program we piloted."

"She did," Maggie confirmed, "and she's got a new program she's trying to get off the ground. Because we did such a good job with *that* one, she wants us to be the first to roll out *this* new one, but it's no pilot. Get this—it's fully funded!"

"That's great, Maggie, truly. Congratulations. But I don't understand what that has to do with me or my credentials."

Maggie laughed, that crazy, deep, throaty sound that had been part of the soundtrack of Lizzie's life for a handful of years. She smiled as nostalgia washed over her. No one laughed quite like Maggie; it was a sound unto itself.

"It has *everything* to do with you, chickadee. The program is a play therapy-based one, set to service foster kids throughout the entire county. I want you to come help me run it."

Lizzie stood there in stunned silence, her palm sweating as it gripped the phone tight to her ear. *Run the program?* Surely she hadn't heard Maggie correctly. She swallowed deeply in an attempt to clear the frog that had taken up residence in her throat. "Did you just say what I think you said?"

"If you think I said that it's time to get your ass back here where you belong, then yes. That's exactly what I said."

"Wow," Lizzie breathed. She was completely stunned. "I'm speechless, Maggie. I never thought ..."

"There was no way you could have. This is brand new. It's not even announced yet. I told Roberta I'd get a team together so she can get the ball rolling. You're the perfect combination of local experience and specific credentials to do this. I need you, Lizzie. Pleeeeeaaaasssee?"

"I ..." Lizzie's gaze wandered to her kitchen table where her lease and the open house flyers sat. She'd already decided not to renew here, and every time she thought about moving somewhere else in town, a knot formed deep in her belly. It wasn't that she didn't like Portland. She loved it.

She just happened to love somewhere—*someone*—more.

She dragged her eyes away from the stack of papers and looked to the ceiling, letting loose a silent note of thanks to the universe. She didn't know how it had happened, but somehow, she'd just lucked into the thing she'd wanted most after graduation. The thing she'd never let herself voice aloud for fear of jinxing it.

Finally, after two years, she could go back to River Hill. Back to Max, Mia, and all her friends.

Back to the home of her heart.

"Yes, I'll take it."

LIZZIE SAT ON HER COUCH, her knee bouncing in time to the sound of Max's phone trilling. One ring, two rings, three. Just when she was about to hang up, he answered, sounding like he'd had to run to catch the call in time. "Hey, baby."

"Hi." Lizzie chewed her lip nervously. She didn't know why she was nervous.

Okay, she totally knew why.

While Max had been completely understanding about her applying to grad school a whole state away, once they'd officially gotten together, they'd promised each other not to make any major life decisions without consulting one another first. That went as much for his restaurants as it did the jobs she applied for.

Which, up until tonight had been a non-factor. The

clinic she'd worked for as part of her Master's program was happy to keep her on their payroll as long as they could. After discussing it with Max a few weeks ago, she'd signed another six-month contract with them. She'd already explained this to Maggie, who had assured her it wasn't a problem. The job back in Sonoma didn't start for several months anyway—they were laying the groundwork now for a launch early next year. The timing was actually perfect.

Still …

"Did I get the time wrong again?" he asked, his voice muffled over the sound of a crowd in the background. He was at Frankie's. Of course.

"No. That's all on me this time," she said, a smile seeping into her own voice. No matter what they were doing, they spoke every night at nine o'clock. Whether that meant a phone call that lasted an hour or more, or a few quick texts, they never went more than a day without communicating. Often, Max got the time "wrong" when he couldn't wait to talk to her. She'd been guilty of it a time or two as well.

"Well, you know I'm not complaining," he said. She heard some loud, crackling noises, and she realized he must have put his hand over the speaker to drown out the chaos around him.

But nothing could ever drown out Angelica. "We miss you, Lizzie!"

"The gang all there?"

"Yeah. Taco night."

Mmm, tacos. "Tell everyone I say hello."

"Lizzie says hello," Max repeated dutifully.

"Hey!" That was Naomi.

"Lizzie!" Noah.

"Hiya!" That could only be Maeve.

"When are you coming home?" And Jess.

"Maria misses her Auntie Lizzie." Which meant that had to be Sean.

She smiled, her heart filling with so much warmth she thought it might burst right out of her chest. Max was the great love of her life, but these were her people, too. She couldn't wait to get back to him and Mia, but she was equally excited to see them all, too.

"I miss her, too," she said, feeling her throat catch around the words. She and Max weren't married—heck, they weren't even engaged—so it meant the world to her that Jess and Sean had bestowed the honorific on her anyway.

"Hey," he said, "what's wrong?"

"Nothing's wrong," she said, but her sniffle gave her away.

"Baby. Tell me."

Lizzie pulled another deep breath into her lungs. This was it. She wasn't afraid to tell him that she was coming back to Sonoma, she only wondered what it would mean for their relationship. They were so damn good together, but they'd also spent the majority of their relationship living in two different cities. What if this changed things? Or, what if he wasn't as excited as she was?

There's only one way to find out, she thought, as she let her breath out on one long gust. "I got a job offer today, Max."

"That's fantastic!"

She rubbed her free palm up and down her thigh nervously. It was sweating again. "It really is. I couldn't have written a more perfect job description. It's everything I've been working toward."

He was quiet for a few protracted seconds before saying, "I'm sensing a but ..."

Now or never, Teague.

"I know you only opened Frankie's up here last summer, and it's going so well, but the job—" she took another deep breath "—the job's in Santa Rosa, Max, back at my old agency. I'd be in charge of a child play therapy program there. Maggie—she's running the place now—she just called and asked me to lead it. I know I should have talked to you before I accepted, but like I said, it's everything—"

"—You're coming home?"

"Yes," she whispered. "I'm coming back to Sonoma." She was purposefully careful not to say that she was returning to River Hill. She loved Max, and she knew that he loved her. No man had ever been more demonstrative of that fact than he, but she didn't want to presume too much either.

"Fuck Sonoma," he grumbled. "You're moving back to River Hill. With Mia and me."

She let out the breath she'd held locked in her lungs while she waited for his reply. "I didn't want to assume ..."

He cleared his throat, and when he spoke, his voice was choked with emotion. "Why wouldn't my wife live with me?"

She gasped. "Did you ... can you ... " Her heart was racing, her pulse bouncing in her neck. "Did ... did you just ask me to marry you?"

He chuckled nervously. "Not exactly how I'd planned to do it, but yes. Marry me, Lizzie. Come home to River Hill and be my wife."

Before she could stop them, tears sprung forth and cascaded down her cheeks. She'd hoped that was where their relationship was heading. No woman in her mid-to-late thirties could be in a relationship for over two years and not hope for that outcome. Well, Naomi could, but she was the exception to the rule—in more ways than one. If anyone walked to the beat of her own drum, it was the charming, eccentric artist. But Lizzie was a traditionalist; she'd always wanted a family to call her own. And now she'd have it.

"Yes, Max. I'll marry you!"

He dropped his voice low. "I love you so goddamn much, Lizzie. You don't know how happy this makes me."

She swiped at the tears drying on her face, and

sniffled. "If it's even half as happy as you've made me these past couple of years, then it's very happy indeed."

"I can't wait to see you this weekend."

"Me either," she said with a bright smile. "I was trying to think up a fun way to surprise you when you got here. This has given me a few new ideas."

"What sort of ideas?" he asked quietly, his voice a sexy rumble against her ear.

"You'll just have to wait and see."

"Fuck, I wish it was Thursday already."

"Me too," she sighed, wanting nothing more than to sink into his arms and never let go.

She heard a commotion in the background, and then the sound of him muffling the receiver. "Hey. Can you give me a second?"

"Sure," she said, bouncing in her seat as excitement about the future coursed through her. She was so hopped up on happy endorphins that she couldn't sit still if she wanted to.

Two long minutes later he was back. "If I came up tomorrow would that throw your plans out of whack?"

"You can throw my plans out of whack, anytime, Max. I'll always want to see you."

"All right. I can be there before noon."

"You can?"

"Yup, Angelica just booked me a ticket." He chuckled, and Lizzie could just about picture the fond smile he was wearing. They truly had the best friends in the world.

"I can't wait."

"And Lizzie?"

"Yeah, Max?"

"You might want to get a manicure."

A manicure? "What?"

"I've got a huge fucking diamond burning a hole in my pocket, and our friends are demanding pictures of it on your finger the second I get there."

She laughed, picturing Angelica standing off to the side harassing him, but then his words settled over her and she sucked in a slight breath. "Wait. You already have a ring?"

"Aww, aren't you cute? Baby, I've had this ring since Christmas. Uncle Horatio knows a guy with an antique shop out in Dundee. Mia and I went to pick it out the day I took her to see Santa."

"You did?"

"Lizzie, I've known I was going to marry you since Noah and Angelica's rehearsal dinner. I've been waiting for this weekend for ages."

"You were coming up here to propose?"

He laughed, and the sound set of a flutter of butterflies off in her stomach. She wasn't sure there was a sexier sound in the world than Max Vergaras laughing softly in her ear. "Yeah, I had it all planned out, but when you sounded so unsure about moving back here, I couldn't wait. I needed you to know that you don't just have a *place* in my life. You *are* my life, Lizzie."

"Oh, Max. You're my life, too. You and Mia are everything I've always wanted."

He sniffled quietly. "You too, baby. You too. I'll call you later tonight, okay?"

"Okay. I love you, Max."

"Not as much as I love you."

A few seconds later, her phone went silent, and Lizzie set it down and simply sat there in quiet shock. In the last hour, all of her most fervent wishes had come true. Briefly, she pinched her arm to make sure that she wasn't dreaming, yelping when it burned her skin. No, she was most certainly awake, and this was all definitely real.

As if to underscore that point, her phone buzzed on the coffee table in front of her. She flipped it over, and her mouth split into a big grin. There, on her screen, was a picture of Angelica, Maeve, Jess, and Naomi all giving her a thumbs up. Below the picture, the text read, "IT'S ABOUT TIME!"

Lizzie agreed. It really was.

Once again, Max was at a wedding.

Ben's elbow nudged against his. "You all right?" his best friend murmured.

"Yeah," Max breathed as he watched Lizzie and Mia walk hand-in-hand up the last few steps to meet him in front of the fireplace in The Oakwell Inn's parlor. "I'm perfect."

She was perfect. Her dress was simple, its clean lines emphasizing her figure with just one dramatic swoop of fabric tucked around her shoulders to leave her collarbone bare. Her blonde hair was swept into loose waves kept back from her face by some arcane magic he didn't understand. The warm tones of her skin glowed in the rays of afternoon sun pouring into the windows; like Mother Nature had timed Lizzie's approach to show off her quiet beauty.

She smiled at him as she let go of Mia's hand and turned to face him. Mia stepped back next to Lizzie in the maid of honor position, and Max spared a moment to check on her. She met his eyes with nothing but happiness sparkling there.

They'd chosen a small wedding, so it was just Mia and Ben standing up with them at the makeshift altar, while their friends and family sat on the gold chiavari chairs lining the room. A familiar flicker of sadness hit him when he scanned the small assemblage, noting every one he loved, save his grandparents. They would have wanted to be here—would have tried to make it up from Argentina no matter their health—but they'd both passed on last year. Thank goodness he'd had a chance to introduce Lizzie to them before they'd gone, within days of each other. He, Lizzie, and Mia had all flown down last Christmas, and they'd spent a cozy holiday sifting through old pictures and visiting his favorite haunts from his childhood. He'd added five new dishes to Frankie's menu when he'd gotten back, inspired by everything they'd eaten.

Now his family was down to just him and Mia, and Lizzie, of course. Her uncles were here, too; Uncle Horatio was sobbing into an embroidered handkerchief, while Uncle Jonathan patted his back soothingly.

They were delightful, and Mia adored them as much as Lizzie had as a child. There had been several visits back and forth to their home once Lizzie had moved back to River Hill permanently.

It had taken them another full year to get here, in front of these people in this room. Between the six months Lizzie had spent wrapping everything up in Portland, and the time it had taken them to get settled in to living together, they'd barely had time to plan anything—even with their friends' extraordinary help. She'd been busy with her new job, and he'd been opening up yet another restaurant, while also trying to train managers for his franchises. So far, nobody was as good as Wendy, but he had high hopes. She still ruled the kitchen at the original Frankie's with an iron fist, but she'd taken a break today to oversee the catering here. He hadn't even tried to argue with her.

Max brought his attention back to the proceedings. The justice of the peace was almost done with his part; it was nearly his turn.

He lifted a hand to his breast pocket, feeling the paper inside it crinkle. He'd written out his vows just to be safe, but here, in the moment, he knew he didn't need them. He'd memorized them the night he wrote them, pouring his heart out on paper. He wasn't normally much of a scribe—there was a reason he liked to communicate with food, not words—but his vows had been so easy to pen it had been like sautéing onions in butter, just so … simple and good. Lizzie was easy to love, and it was easy to tell her so.

"Go ahead, Max," the officiant said with a beatific smile.

He took a deep breath, and closed his fingers around Lizzie's outstretched hands, two charms dangling from her wrist. Last night he'd gifted her with another charm to join the anchor he'd bought her years before, this one a small key. She'd unlocked his heart, and opened up his whole world.

"Lizzie," he began. Then he stopped, cleared his throat, and started again, ignoring the *whuff* of Ben's quiet chuckle behind him. "Lizzie. From the moment I met you, you've been a beacon. You've shined your light into every part of my life, from unexpected parenthood to friendship, to restaurant menus and new ideas. I can't imagine being without you. I want you to know that I promise to spend every day thinking of you. It won't be hard, because I already do. Sometimes you're very distracting." He held up the bandaged pinky finger of his right hand, the result of a sloppy knife cut two days ago, and heard Wendy's distinct whoop of laughter at the back of the room. "I promise to always support you in whatever you do, and bring snacks to your office whenever you want them." Another chuckle swept the room. "I promise to put your name on all of my menus—" He already had, in fact. Every single one of his restaurants served a dish named after her, and he had more planned. "And to watch every movie on your list of must-see historical dramas." This was commitment, after all. He plunged forward. "I promise to spend every moment grateful that we found each other, and made our way through every complication life could throw at us, and to always remember how very lucky I am that you chose me, and stuck with me. I'll try to be the best husband I can be, and the best friend you deserve."

Lizzie's eyes glimmered with happy tears as she looked up at him, fingers tightening around his. She licked her lips, and he resisted all of the wildly inappropriate urges it gave him while she took her own deep breath and started to speak. "Max. You've been there for me in more ways than I can ever count, and I promise to return the favor every day of my life. You've helped me become a better person with your kindness, your goodness, and your grace— and let's not forget the food."

Somebody in the audience muttered "Amen." It might have been Angelica, but he wasn't sure, since he couldn't tear his eyes away from his bride.

Lizzie went on. "You're the best person I know. I wake up every day grateful to you for being in my life, and thankful that we found the strength together to work hard to get here. I promise to love you without measure, and to listen to all of your ideas, and to taste test all of your new menu items, even the weird ones." The tapioca-based salad dressing had *not* gone over well. "I promise to catch you if you fall, and fly alongside you when you soar. I promise to go to every restaurant opening and every school show." Mia hiccuped a small giggle, then sniffled, and Lizzie reached back with her free hand to clasp Mia's fingers briefly. "I'll try to be the best wife I can be, and the best friend that you deserve, too."

Ben nudged Max's elbow, and he managed to tear his eyes away from Lizzie's mesmerizing gaze long enough to realize that he was being handed the rings. He plucked the band that matched the tear-shaped diamond he'd slipped on her finger a year ago off the little pillow and slid it on with shaking hands. Hers were rock-steady as she did the same with the plain titanium band that went onto his finger. There was a silicone version waiting for him at home that he'd use in the kitchen, too. She'd ordered it as a surprise and shown it to him this morning, and he'd expressed his gratitude so thoroughly they'd barely made it to their own wedding on time.

Now, the officiant was pronouncing them man and wife, and Lizzie was beaming up at him, and Max didn't even bother to wait for permission before he gathered her into his arms and sealed his lips to hers. He lost himself in the kiss, the fingers of his free hand still tangled in hers while he brought his newly-ringed hand up to cup her cheek. He slid his thumb along her jaw as he tasted the rich sweetness of her lips, and she swayed closer to him.

Eventually somebody cleared their throat loudly

enough for him to notice. Reluctantly, he pulled away from Lizzie. Mia's giggles were loud enough to be heard throughout the room, and he grinned at his niece as he wrapped his arm around Lizzie and turned them to face the audience. On her other side, Lizzie reached out to gather the girl against her with her free arm, and they presented themselves as a united family to their applauding friends.

As they made their way through the crowd, Max let his gaze linger on all of his friends, marveling at the changes the years had brought to River Hill. There were Noah and Angelica, still the backbone of their group after all this time. They'd made so many memories together since Angelica had first come to River Hill to renovate The Oakwell. And the two of them were on to making more; they'd just finished building a barn that linked Noah's vineyard to Angelica's inn, making it the new tasting room for Stonewell Vineyards. They'd filmed the entire build for Angelica's TV show, of course. Her filming schedule was still rigorous these days, but Noah often travelled with her, perched behind the cameras with their tiny six-month-old son in a carrier slung about his large torso.

And speaking of babies, there were Maeve and Jess, side by side as Ben went to rejoin his wife. Somehow, the two women had conspired to get pregnant at the same time, Maeve with her first and Jess with a sibling for little Maria, and they were deeply smug about the whole thing. They reached out from either side to embrace Lizzie as closely as they could behind nearly eight months of baby bump. Max grinned at Ben and Sean, the former still looking a little dazed at the idea of fatherhood and the latter deeply comfortable with it. Maria was already learning to bake alongside her father, although thus far nobody had been subjected to her creations. Not until her tiny hands learned to measure a little better, anyway.

Naomi and Iain completed the crowd, barreling right in to join the giant group hug that was forming. They'd happily sponsored Mia's most recent art excursion, which had involved tours of several different art schools. She was barely thirteen, so Max hardly thought she was ready to think about college, but Naomi had described some of the studios so glowingly that Mia had been completely unstoppable in her desire to visit. She'd wound up applying and being accepted to several art-based summer programs for young adults, and Naomi was nearly as smug as Jess and Maeve were. Iain, of course, just grinned cheerfully at anybody and everybody around, and somehow people found themselves doing what he wanted them to do.

Which was how Max had been talked into his latest venture—a Frankie's-branded marketplace where the vendors and distributors he'd worked with for the last ten years could sell some of the amazing local products he used in all of his restaurants. Ben had brought the lease for the space over last night, and he already had contracts in hand from Iain and Noah to sell their wares. Buzz about the market was growing, and he'd had inquiries from other vendors and restaurant owners all over Sonoma. He also had a strong suspicion that Angelica had something up her sleeve regarding the renovation of the space he was planning to use.

Today, this moment right here, was the culmination of all of his years in River Hill, with the people he loved, and Lizzie beside him to make it all happen. He couldn't imagine doing it any other way than with this special group of friends beside him. He couldn't imagine doing *anything* without them, honestly—this wedding included.

And so here they were, gathered together again as they would continue to gather for the rest of their lives, love and laughter ringing out into the room as friends became family one more time. This was just the beginning of their forever, and Max couldn't wait to see what came next.

The End

ACKNOWLEDGMENTS

From Rebecca:

Back in 2017, I stumbled upon some stock photos of hot men doing hot things, and an idea was born. Never could I have predicted what an amazing experience writing this series with Jamaila would be. Whether it was long car rides together where we plotted (!!) our characters' journeys, or (literal) long walks on the beach, it's been a joy. They say to write what you love and this job will never feel like work, and I can say from the bottom of my heart that is true for the time we spent writing this series. Thanks, as always, to my husband for supporting me and believing in my talent. Every time I've wanted to chase a trend, he reminds me about what we've accomplished with our Vintner, Distiller, Baker, Barista, and now our Chef, and why I love writing stories about good food, good booze, and good people. Thank you to the many professionals who weighed in on these characters so that they were as authentic as possible, especially Brad, Danny, Grady, and Ana at Mercury Vineyards, who patiently answered all my questions about wine making in Sonoma County from the outset of this series. And finally, many thanks to Anthony Bourdain, who made me want to write about a badass chef with a big heart in the first place. You may be gone, but your legacy will never be forgotten.

From Jamaila:

This series has come a long way and owes so much to so many people, most especially my co-writer Rebecca; after fifteen years, six houses, two children, three cats, and five books, we're still friends and I'm so grateful. A huge thank you to the locked Twitter crew, for making me (and my characters!) appreciate the joys of therapy; thanks as always to my family, especially my children, who go to kindergarten and tell everybody that mommy writes romance books. And a very special thank you to the various chefs, restaurant owners, therapists, and social workers who have given us advice about this book, including Lance Cook and his crew at Tino's, Kendra Benesch LCPC, Dr. Sam Marks, and Brandon Dougherty (I hope there are enough swears in here for you, buddy).

WELCOME TO RIVER HILL

THE VINTNER'S VIXEN

Welcome to wine country, where the only thing more intoxicating than the wine is the man who makes it.

With movie roles for "curvy best friend" drying up fast, actress Angelica Travis is happy to leave Hollywood behind to renovate a bed and breakfast in River Hill, the jewel of Northern California's wine country. She's got plans and power tools ready, but an inconvenient attraction to her handsome new neighbor is *not* on the agenda.

Winemaker Noah Bradstone's master plan is right on schedule until construction on the B&B next door threatens his prize-winning grapes. His only choice is to confront his sexy new neighbor, but with her pink toolbelt and quick retorts, she's the single most infuriating woman he's ever met. What's even more infuriating is that he wants her anyway.

Despite their constant bickering, Angelica and Noah discover they have more in common than they thought—including an attraction that burns red hot. But when his past and her future collide, can their love survive a pair of shocking revelations? Better yet, can they survive each other?

THE DISTILLER'S DARLING

Welcome back to River Hill, where love comes when you least expect it.

River Hill is an unlikely place to launch a whiskey empire, but Irishman Iain Brennan's just reckless enough to make it work. And finding out the dark-haired artist he spent one glorious night with lives across town is an added bonus. Since he's never said no to mixing business with pleasure, hiring her to design his labels is the best decision he's made in ages—especially since she's even less interested in a relationship than he is.

Naomi Klein may have put down roots in River Hill, but she's not looking for happily-ever-after. Just the idea of forever gives her hives. Which makes a rootless Irish wanderer in town for three months the perfect fling. The fact that he's happy to let her focus on her art makes spending time with him even more appealing. And shocking her society mother? Just a bonus.

But as cozy autumn nights turn into lazy winter mornings, Iain and Naomi realize they've done the unthinkable and fallen in love! Neither are ready to settle down, but settling for a life without the other is out of the question. Or is it?

THE BAKER'S BEAUTY

Welcome back to River Hill, where life is a little bit sweet and a whole lotta spicy.

After tragedy struck, Sean Amory left L.A. to come home to River Hill to work at his family's bakery. The familiar surroundings soothe his raw nerves while the gorgeous brunette who jogs past every morning has another effect entirely. And when she helps him out of a bind, he learns Jess is even sweeter than the apple fritters he's become famous for.

Former beauty queen Jessica Casillas-Moore hasn't eaten carbs since she was fourteen, but that doesn't stop her from jogging past The Breadery every morning. And when she meets the handsome baker who works there, Sean is every bit as mouthwatering as the pastries he serves. And so much better for her waistline.

But between her family's disapproval and his haunting past, the odds seem stacked against them. Can Sean and Jess learn to trust in each other and their growing love, or is their relationship a recipe for disaster?

THE BARISTA'S BELOVED

Return to River Hill, where the coffee isn't the only thing that'll leave you buzzing.

It's been months since whiskey maker Maeve Brennan has been on a date, and she's coming dangerously close to giving up on men altogether—until she crosses paths with River Hill's sexy new barista. But Ben's made it clear he only wants to be friends, so Maeve will definitely stop fantasizing about his forearms. Probably. Maybe.

Former lawyer Ben Worthington never thought he'd be living above his best friend's garage and slinging coffee, but there's a lot about his life that doesn't make sense. Like his attraction to the town's beloved distiller. But since Maeve's made it clear she doesn't have time for romance, Ben will stop dreaming about her naked. Soon. Eventually.

But when the youth center where Maeve volunteers comes under fire from a big-city developer, Ben realizes he's exactly the type of hero she needs. He just hopes she can live with his take-no-prisoners approach to winning, because he's pretty sure he can't live without her.

THE CHEF'S CUTIE

Take a final trip to River Hill, where the kitchen isn't the only place things are heating up.

Chef Max Vergaras's culinary star is rising, but when his orphaned niece comes to live with him, expanding his restaurant empire is put on the back burner. He's ill equipped to handle raising a nine year old, especially under the watchful eye of Elizabeth Teague, the social services caseworker assigned to them. His life has never been more complicated, which includes his feelings for the blonde beauty: she's everything he wants—and everything he can't have. And since Lizzie holds his family's future in the palm of her hand, all of his thoughts about how she fits seamlessly into his life need to go on the back burner, too. Just as soon as he figures out how to get her out of his dreams.

Lizzie Teague has an important job to do, and she can't get distracted by one case—even if Mia's uncle Max has a way with food that has her thinking about things that definitely aren't on the menu. But with her career and reputation on the line, she has to remember why she took this job in the first place ... and it certainly wasn't to fall in love with her clients. No matter how loveable the sexy, charismatic chef and his sweet, young niece might be. So she'll keep her mind on the job and out of the gutter—just as soon as she can get her heart on board with that plan.

Max and Lizzie could lose everything if they give in to temptation. But what if it's possible for them to gain even more? What would they risk when love—and family—is on the line?

ABOUT THE AUTHORS

Rebecca Norinne and Jamaila Brinkley have been friends for almost fifteen years. Separately, they write contemporary romance and historical fantasy romance; together, they created the enchanting world of River Hill.

In this charming Northern California town, Norinne and Brinkley combined the interests that made them friends in the first place—great food, delicious wine, and a pinch of home renovation—and added in the spicy romance they love.

Rebecca lives in Massachusetts with her husband, and Jamaila lives in Maryland with her husband and twin children. They text each other a lot.

Steamy Standalones
Protect Me
Lucky Star
The Ties That Bind
Return To Me

ALSO BY JAMAILA BRINKLEY

THE WIZARDS OF LONDON SERIES
Thieves' Honor

Witch's Stone

Captain's Lady

THE GALIPP FILES
The Star of Anatolia

The Mathematical Gambit

The Portrait Problem

The Demigod Dilemma

(part of the Caught in Crystal Gaslamp anthology)